The Lemonade war

by Jacqueline Davies

SCHOLASTIC INC.
New York Toronto London Auckland
Sydney Mexico City New Delhi Hong Kong

ISBN 978-0-545-46798-8

20 19 18 17 16 15   14 15/0

Printed in the U.S.A.   23

This edition first printing, May 2012

The text of this book is set in Guardi.

Pronunciations are reproduced by permission from
The American Heritage Dictionary of the English Language, Fourth Edition,
© 2006 by Houghton Mifflin Company.

For Tom, Kim, and Leslie.
All roads lead back.

Contents

Chapter 1
SLUMP

slump (slŭmp) n. A drop in the activity of a business or the economy.

Evan lay on his back in the dark, throwing the baseball up in a straight line and catching it in his bare hands. *Thwap. Thwap.* The ball made a satisfying sound as it slapped his palm. His legs flopped in a V. His arms stretched up to the ceiling. And the thought that if he missed he'd probably break his nose made the game *just* interesting enough to keep going.

On the floor above he heard footsteps—his mother's—and then a long, loud scraping-groaning sound. He stopped throwing the ball to listen. His mother was dragging something heavy across the kitchen floor. Probably the broken air conditioner.

A week ago, right at the beginning of the heat wave, the air conditioner in his mother's attic office had broken. The man from Sears had installed a brand-new one but left the old one sitting right in the middle of the kitchen floor. The Treskis had been walking around it all week.

Scra-a-a-ape. Evan stood up. His mom was strong, but this was a two-person job. Hopefully she wouldn't ask him why he was hiding in the dark basement. And hopefully Jessie wouldn't be in the kitchen at all. He'd been avoiding her for two days now, and it was getting harder by the minute. The house just wasn't that big.

Evan had his hand on the railing when the scraping noise stopped. He heard footsteps fading to silence. She'd given up. *Probably the heat,* he thought. It was that kind of weather: giving-up kind of weather.

He went back to lying on the floor.

Thwap. Thwap.

Then he heard the basement door open. *Psssshhh.* Evan caught the ball and froze.

"Evan?" Jessie's voice sounded echo-y in the darkness. "Evan? You down there?"

Evan held his breath. He lay completely still. The only thing that moved was the pins-and-needles prickling in his fingers.

He heard the door start to close—*long breath out*—but then it stopped and opened again. Footsteps on the carpeted stairs. A black outline of Jessie standing on the bottom step with daylight squirting all around her. Evan didn't move a muscle.

"Evan? Is that you?" Jessie took one short step into the basement. "Is that . . . ? She inched her way toward him, then kicked him with her bare foot.

"Hey! Watch it, would ya?" said Evan, swatting her leg. He suddenly felt stupid lying there in the dark.

"I thought you were a sleeping bag," she said. "I couldn't see. What are you doing down here? How come the lights are off?"

"It's too hot with the lights on," he said. He talked in a flat voice, trying to sound like the most boring person on the whole planet. If he kept it up, Jessie might just leave him alone.

"Mom's back in her office," said Jessie, lying down on the couch. *"Working."* She groaned as she said the word.

Evan didn't say anything. He went back to throwing the ball. Straight up. Straight down. Maybe silence would get Jessie to leave. He was starting to feel words piling up inside him, crowding his lungs, forcing out all the air. It was like having a chestful of bats, beating their wings, fighting to get out.

"She tried to move the air conditioner, but it's too heavy," said Jessie.

Evan tightened up his lips. *Go away,* he thought. *Go away before I say something mean.*

"It's gonna be hot *a-a-a-all* week," Jessie continued. "In the nineties. All the way up 'til Labor Day."

Thwap. Thwap.

"So, whaddya wanna do?" Jessie asked.

Scream, thought Evan. Jessie never got it when you were giving her the Big Freeze. She just went right on acting as if everything were great. It made it really hard to tell her to bug off without telling her to *BUG OFF!* Whenever Evan did that, he felt bad.

"So, whaddya wanna do?" Jessie asked again, nudging him with her foot.

It was a direct question. Evan had to answer it or explain why he wouldn't. And he couldn't get into *that*. It was too . . . too complicated. Too hurtful.

"Huh? So, whaddya wanna do?" she asked for the third time.

"Doin' it," said Evan.

"Nah, come on. For real."

"For real," he said.

"We could ride our bikes to the 7-Eleven," she said.

"No money," he said.

"You just got ten dollars from Grandma for your birthday."

"Spent it," said Evan.

"On what?"

"Stuff," Evan said.

"Well, I've got . . . well . . . " Jessie's voice dribbled down to nothing.

Evan stopped throwing the ball and looked at her. "What?"

Jessie pulled her legs tight to her chest. "Nothin'," she said.

"Right," said Evan. He knew that Jessie had money. Jessie always had money squirreled away in her lock box. But that didn't mean she was going to share it. Evan went back to throwing the baseball. He felt a tiny flame of anger shoot up and lick his face.

Thwap. Thwap.

"We could build a fort in the woods," said Jessie.

"Too hot."

"We could play Stratego."

"Too boring."

"We could build a track and race marbles."

"Too stupid!"

A thin spider web of sweat draped itself over his forehead, spreading into his hair. With every throw, he told himself, *It's not her fault.* But he could feel his anger growing. He started popping his elbow to put a little more juice on the ball. It was flying a good four feet into the air every time. Straight up. Straight down.

Pop. Thwap. Pop. Thwap.

The bats in his chest were going nuts.

"What is the matter with you?" asked Jessie. "You've been so weird the last couple of days."

Aw, man, here they come.

"I just don't wanna play a dumb game like Stratego," he said.

"You *like* Stratego. I only picked that because it's *your* favorite game. I was being *nice,* in case you hadn't noticed."

"Look. There are only six days left of summer, and I'm not going to waste them playing a dumb game." Evan felt his heartbeat speed up. Part of him wanted to stuff a sock in his mouth, and part of him wanted to deck his sister. "It's a stupid game and it's for babies and I don't want to play a stupid baby game."

Pop. Thwap. Pop. Thwap.

"Why are you being so mean?"

Evan knew he was being mean, and he hated being mean, especially to her. But he couldn't help it. He was so angry and so humiliated and so full of bats, there was nothing else he *could* be. Except alone. And she'd taken even that away from him. "You're the genius," he said. "You figure it out."

Good. That would shut her up. For once! Evan watched the ball fly in the air.

"Is this because of the letter?" Jessie asked.

Crack.

Evan had taken his eyes off the ball for one second, just for one second, and the ball came crashing down on his nose.

"Crud! Oh, CRUD!" He curled over onto his side, grabbing his nose with both hands. There was a blinding, blooming pain right behind his eyes that was quickly spreading to the outer edges of his skull.

"Do you want some ice?" he heard Jessie ask in a calm voice.

"Whaddya think?" he shouted.

"Yeah?" She stood up.

"No, I don't want any stupid ice." The pain was starting to go away, like a humungous wave that crashes with a lot of noise and spray but then slowly fizzles away into nothing. Evan rolled to a sitting position and took his hands away from his nose. With his thumb and index finger, he started to pinch the bridge. Was it still in a straight line?

Jessie peered at his face in the dim light. "You're not bleeding," she said.

"Yeah, well, it *hurts!*" he said. "A lot!"

"It's not broken," she said.

"You don't know that," he said. "You don't know *everything,* you know. You think you do, but you *don't.*"

"It's not even swollen. You're making a big deal out of nothing."

Evan held his nose with one hand and hit his sister's knee with the other. Then he picked up the baseball and struggled to his feet. "Leave me alone.

I came down here to get away from you and you just had to follow. You ruin everything. You ruined my summer and now you're going to ruin school. I hate you." When he got to the bottom of the steps, he threw the baseball down in disgust.

Thud.

Chapter 2
Breakup

breakup (brāk′up′) n. Dissolution of a unit, an organization, or a group of organizations. The Justice Department sometimes forces the breakup of a large corporation into several smaller companies.

Jessie didn't get it. She just didn't get it.

What was Evan's problem?

He'd been acting like a weirdo for two days now. And it was two days ago that the letter had arrived. But why would he be so upset about that letter?

This is a puzzle, Jessie told herself. *And I'm good at puzzles.* But it was a puzzle about feelings, and Jessie knew that feelings were her weakest subject.

Jessie sat in the cool darkness of the basement and thought back to Monday, the day the letter had come. Everything had been normal. She and Evan were putting together a lemonade stand in the driveway when the mailman walked up and handed Jessie a bundle of letters. Evan never bothered to look at the mail, but Jessie was always entering contests and expecting to win, so she flipped through the letters right away.

"Boring. Boring. Boring," said Jessie as each letter flashed by. "Hey, something from school. Addressed to Mom." She held up a plain white envelope. "What do you think it is?"

"Dunno," said Evan. He was in the garage, uncovering the small wooden table they usually used for a stand. It was buried under two sno-tubes, two boogie boards, and the garden hose. Jessie watched while Evan gave a mighty pull and lifted the table up over his head. *Wow, he's gotten so big,* thought Jessie, remembering what Mom had said about Evan's growth spurt. Sometimes Jessie felt like Evan was growing twice as fast as she was.

Growing up. Growing away.

"It looks important," said Jessie. *It looks like bad news* is what she thought in her head. Was there a problem? A complaint? A mix-up? All the nervousness she'd been feeling about skipping to fourth grade suddenly burbled up inside her.

"This table's really dirty," said Evan. "Do you think we can just cover it with a lot of cups and the pitcher and no one will notice?"

Jessie looked. The table was streaked with black. "No."

Evan groaned.

"I'll clean it," said Jessie. Evan had only agreed to have a lemonade stand because it was one of *her* favorite things to do. The least she could do for him was clean the gunk off the table. "Maybe," she said, holding up the envelope again, "they're postponing school? Maybe the first day isn't going to be next Tuesday? Ya think?"

That got Evan's attention. "Let's ask Mom to open it," he said.

Up in the humming cool of her office, Mrs.

Treski read the letter through once. "Well," she said. "This is a curve ball." She looked right at Evan. Jessie thought her face looked worried. "Evan, you and Jessie are going to be in the same class this year. You'll both have Mrs. Overton."

Jessie felt relief flood her entire body. The same class! If she could have wished for one thing in the whole world, that's what she would have wished for. She would be with Evan, and Evan would make everything easier. He would introduce her to all those fourth-graders. He would show them all that she was okay. Not some puny second-grader who didn't really belong.

But Evan didn't look happy. He looked angry. "Why?" he asked in an almost-shouting voice.

Mrs. Treski scanned the letter. "Well, the classes were small to start with. And now some of the fourth-graders they thought would be attending aren't because they're moving or switching to private schools. So they need to combine the two small classes into one bigger class."

"That is so unfair," said Evan. "I wanted Mrs.

Scobie. And I don't want—" He looked at Jessie. "That is *so* unfair!"

Jessie was surprised. This was great news. Why didn't Evan see that? They always had fun together at home. Now they could have fun in school, too. "It'll be fun," she said to Evan.

"It will not be fun," said Evan. "School. Isn't. Fun." And then he stomped downstairs and locked himself in his room for the rest of the afternoon. They never finished the lemonade stand.

And here it was, two days later, and Evan was still all locked up, even though he wasn't in his room. He wouldn't talk to her, and he wouldn't play with her.

So Jessie went up to her room and did what she always did when she was upset or angry or sad or confused. She started reading *Charlotte's Web*. She had read the book about a hundred times.

She was at the good part, the happy part. Wilbur had just been named "some pig," and he was getting all kinds of attention from the Zuckermans and the whole town. But Jessie couldn't settle into

that happy feeling, the one that usually came when
Charlotte said:

> I dare say my trick will work and Wilbur's
> life can be saved.

Instead, she kept noticing an unhappy feeling
tap-tap-tapping on her shoulder. And it wasn't the
unhappy feeling that came from knowing that
Charlotte was going to die on page 171.

It was Evan. She couldn't stop thinking about
what he had said.

Jessie could only remember one other time that
Evan had said "I hate you" to her. Grandma had
been over and Evan needed help with his math
homework. He had that frustrated, screwed-up-
mouth look that he sometimes got with math or
spelling or writing reports. Mom called it his "he's-
a-gonna-blow!" look. But Grandma couldn't help
him because it was "all Greek" to her. So Jessie had
shown him how to do each problem. Well, she'd
just sort of jumped in and done the problems for

him. That was helping, wasn't it? Grandma had called her a girl genius, but Evan had ripped his paper in half and run upstairs, shouting "I hate you!" just before slamming his door. That was last year.

Jessie rested the book on her stomach and stared at the ceiling. People were confusing. She'd rather do a hundred math problems than try to figure out someone else's mixed-up feelings, any day of the week. That's why she and Evan got along so well. He'd just tell her, straight out, "I'm mad at you because you ate the last Rice Krispie's Treat." And then she could say, "Sorry. Hey, I've got some Starburst in my room. You want them?" And that would be that.

Evan was a straight shooter.

Not like the girls at school, the ones who had started that club. She rolled over onto her side to get away from *those* thoughts.

Across the room, against the opposite wall, she noticed the three pieces of foam core her mom had bought for Jessie's Labor Day project. Every year, the Rotary Club sponsored a competition for kids to see who could come up with the best display related to the holiday. This was the first year Jessie was old enough to participate, and she had begged her mom to buy foam core and gel pens and fluorescent paper and special stickers for her display. She was determined to win the prize money: a hundred dollars! But she hadn't been able to come up with a single idea that seemed good enough. So here it was, just five days before the competition, and the foam core was still completely blank.

Jessie reached for her book. She didn't want to think about the girls at school and she didn't want to think about the competition. She started reading again.

Wilbur and Charlotte were at the fair, and Charlotte was beginning to show her age. Jessie read the words that Wilbur said to his best friend.

I'm awfully sorry to hear that you're feeling poorly, Charlotte. Perhaps if you spin a web and catch a couple of flies you'll feel better.

Well, the second part didn't apply at all, but Jessie imagined herself saying the first line: *I'm awfully sorry to hear that you're feeling poorly, Evan.* It sounded about right. At least it would show him that she cared, and Jessie knew that this was important when someone was feeling upset. She decided to go downstairs and give it a try. She would do just about anything to get Evan back to the way he was before the letter.

Jessie looked in the kitchen and the backyard—no Evan. She was halfway down the steps to the basement when she heard a noise coming from the garage. She opened the door and felt the full heat of the day on her skin. It was like some giant had blown his hot, stinky breath on her.

In the garage, she found Evan and Scott Spencer. *Weird,* she thought. *Evan doesn't even like Scott Spencer.* They'd been on-again, off-again friends from kindergarten. But ever since Scott had purposely put Evan's bike helmet under the wheel of the Treskis' minivan so that Mrs. Treski ran over it when she backed out, the friendship had definitely been *off*.

19

Jessie looked from Evan to Scott and back again. Now she had no idea what to say. *I'm awfully sorry to hear that you're feeling poorly, Evan*, didn't seem to make much sense when Evan was obviously having fun with his friend. She tried to think of something else to say. All she could come up with was "What're you doing?"

The boys were bent over a piece of cardboard. Evan was writing letters with a skinny red felt-tipped pen. The purple cooler was in the middle of the garage and two plastic chairs were stacked on top of it. On the top chair was a brown paper bag.

"Nothing," said Evan, not looking up.

Jessie walked over to the boys and peered over Evan's shoulder.

L eminade
50 ¢

She said, "You spelled *lemonade* wrong. It's an *o*, not an *i*." But she thought, *Oh, good! A lemonade stand. My favorite thing to do!*

The boys didn't say anything. Jessie saw Evan's mouth tighten up.

"You want me to make the lemonade?" she asked.

"Already made," said Evan.

"I could decorate the sign," she said. "I'm good at drawing butterflies and flowers and things."

Scott snorted. "*Huh!* We don't want *girl* stuff like that on our sign!"

"Do you want to use my lock box to keep the money in? It's got a tray with separate compartments for all the different coins."

"Nope," said Evan, still working on the sign.

"Well," she said, looking around. "I can clean the table for you." The small wooden table, still covered in black streaks, was pushed up against the bikes.

"We're not using it," said Evan.

"But we always use the table for a stand," said Jessie.

Evan pushed his face in her direction. "We don't want it."

Jessie took a couple of steps back. Her insides felt runny, like a fried egg that hasn't cooked enough. She knew she should just go back into the house. But for some reason her legs wouldn't move. She stood still, her bare feet rooted to the cool cement.

Scott whispered something to Evan and the two boys laughed, low and mean. Jessie swayed toward the door, but her feet stayed planted. She couldn't stand it that Evan wanted to be with Scott—who was a real jerk—more than her.

"Hey," she said. "I bet you need change. I've got a ton. You could have all my change. You know, as long as you pay it back at the end of the day."

"Don't need it," said Evan.

"Yeah, you do," insisted Jessie. "You always need change, especially in the beginning. You'll lose sales if you can't make change."

Evan capped the pen with a loud *snap!* and stuck it in his pocket. "Scott's bankrolling us. His mom keeps a change jar, so we've got plenty."

The boys stood up. Evan held the sign for Scott to read, turning his back on Jessie. "Awesome," said Scott.

Jessie knew that the sign was not awesome. The letters were too small and thin to read from a distance. (Evan should have used a fat marker instead of a skinny felt-tipped pen. Everybody knew that!) There weren't any pretty decorations to attract customers. And the word *lemonade* was spelled wrong. Why wouldn't Evan take a *little* help from her? She just wanted to help.

Scott turned to her and said, "Are you really going to be in fourth grade this year?"

Jessie's back stiffened. "Yep," she said.

"Wow. That is so freaky."

"Is not," she said, sticking her chin out.

"Is too," said Scott. "I mean, you're a *second*-grader and now you're gonna be a *fourth*-grader. That's just messed up."

Jessie looked at Evan, but he was busy taping the sign to the cooler.

"Lots of people skip grades," said Jessie. "It's not that big a deal."

"It's completely weird!" said Scott. "I mean, you miss everything from a whole year. You miss the whole unit on Antarctica, and that was the best.

And the field trip to the aquarium. And the thing where we sent letters all over the country. Remember that, Evan? You got that letter from Alaska. That was so cool!"

Evan nodded, but he didn't look up.

"It's not that big a deal," said Jessie again, her voice stretched tight like a rubber band.

"It's like you miss a year of your life," Scott said. "It's like you're gonna *die* a whole year earlier than the rest of us because you never had third grade."

Jessie felt cold and hot at the same time. Part of her wanted to yell, "That doesn't make any sense!" But the other part of her felt so *freakish*—like Scott had just noticed she had three legs.

Evan stood up and tossed the paper bag to Scott. Then he grabbed the plastic chairs with one hand. "Come on. Let's go." He reached down to grab one handle of the cooler. Scott grabbed the other, and together they lifted it and began to walk out of the garage.

"Hey, Evan," said Jessie, calling to their backs. "Can I come, too?"

"No," he said, without turning around.

"Come on. Please? I'll be a big help. I can do lots of things—"

"You're too young," he said sharply. "You're just a baby."

The boys walked out.

You're just a baby.

Jessie couldn't believe Evan had said that. After all the stuff they'd done together. And he was only *fourteen months* older than she was. Hardly even a full year. She was about to yell back something really harsh, something stinging and full of bite, like *Oh, yeah?*, when she heard Scott say to Evan, "Man, I can't believe you have to be in the same class as your little sister. If that happened to me, I'd move to South America."

"Yeah, tell me about it," replied Evan, crossing the street.

The words died on Jessie's lips. She watched Evan walking away, getting smaller and smaller.

He was deserting her.

He *wasn't* going to stand by her at school. He

wasn't going to smooth the way for her. He was going to be on the *other* side, with all of *them,* looking down on her. Telling everyone that she was too young to be part of the crowd. Telling everyone that she didn't belong.

"Fine for you, Evan Treski," she said as she marched into the house, her fists balled up at her sides. "I don't need *you*. I don't need *you* to have fun. I don't need *you* to run a lemonade stand. And I don't need *you* to make friends in the fourth grade."

Halfway up the stairs, she stopped and shouted, "And I am *not* a baby!"

Chapter 3
Joint Venture

joint venture (joint věn′chər) n. Two or more people joining forces to sell a certain amount of goods or to work on a single project. When the goods are sold or the project is finished, the joint venture ends.

"Your sister is really—"

"Shut up," said Evan.

"Huh?"

"Just shut up. She's okay. She just . . . she doesn't . . . look, she's okay. So just shut up."

"Y'okay," said Scott, holding up his free hand to show he meant peace.

Evan was getting abused on both sides. The

heavy cooler was banging against his inside leg with every step. And the plastic chairs were scraping against his outside leg. *Bruised and bloodied,* he thought to himself. *All for the fun of hanging out with Scott Spencer.*

Why couldn't Jack have been home? Or Ryan? And why did Adam have to be on the Cape this week? It stunk.

"How far are we walking?" grunted Scott.

"Just to the corner." Evan watched as drops of sweat fell off his face and landed on the hot sidewalk.

"We shoulda stayed in the driveway. It was shaded."

"The corner's better. Trust me," said Evan.

He remembered when Jessie had said the same words to him last summer. They were setting up a lemonade stand together, and Evan had been grumbling about dragging the cooler across the street and down two houses, just like Scott. But Jessie had insisted. "There's sidewalk on this side," she'd said. "So we'll get the foot traffic coming in both directions. And people in cars coming around the curve will have time to see us and slow down. Besides, there are a bunch of little kids on the side street and their mothers won't want them crossing Damon Road. The corner's better. Trust me."

And she was right. They'd made a ton of money that afternoon.

It took ten seconds to set up the lemonade stand. Evan unfolded the chairs and set one on each side of the cooler. Scott tilted the sign toward the street for maximum effect. Then they both sat down.

"Man, is it hot," said Evan. He took off his baseball cap and wiped the sweat from his face with his shirt. Then he grabbed an ice cube from the cooler, balanced it on his head, and stuck his cap back on.

"Yeah," said Scott. "I'm thirsty." He reached into the paper bag and pulled out a cup. It was one of those large red plastic cups that vendors use at professional baseball games. Then Scott took one of the pitchers from the cooler and filled the cup to the brim with lemonade.

"Hey, not so much," said Evan, pouring himself a cup, too, but only partway. He glugged down half his drink. *Not bad*, he thought, though he noticed a dead fruit fly floating on the top. His mom had been battling a mad fruit-fly infestation ever since the weather had turned really warm. The kitchen sink area, where they kept their fruit bowl, was dotted with tiny, feathery fruit-fly corpses.

Scott drained his cup and tossed it on the ground. "Aahhh," he said, satisfied. "That was good. I'm gonna have another."

Evan reached for the trashed cup and stowed it under his seat. "Nah, c'mon, Scott. You're gonna drink all our profits if you do that." He stretched his legs out by putting his feet on top of the cooler. "Just chill."

"I'm gonna chill by having another cup," said Scott.

There it was. That mean bite in Scott's voice. Evan's shoulders tensed up.

"Move your feet," said Scott. "It's hot out here."

"Dude, you're—" Evan sat up expectantly and looked down the street. "Hey, here comes our first customer."

A mother pushing a double stroller came into view. At the same time, one of the kindergartners from down the street rode her bike up, noticed the sign, and quickly pedaled back to her house. Within five minutes, there was a small crowd of neighborhood kids and pedestrians buying lemonade from the stand.

Evan let Scott handle all the money while he took care of the pouring and the "sweet talk." That's what his mother called it when a salesperson chatted her up. "Trust me," she had once told Evan and Jessie. "Buying something is only *half* about getting something. The other half is all about human contact." Mrs. Treski knew about these things because she was a public relations consultant. She'd even written a booklet called *Ten Bright Ideas to Light Up Your Sales* for one of her clients. And Evan was like her: He was good at talking with people. Even grownups. It was easy for him. So he kept the conversation flowing, along with the lemonade. People hung around. Most of them bought a second cup before they left.

Evan was so busy, he almost didn't notice Jessie flying out of the garage on her bike and riding down the street toward town. *Good riddance,* he thought—but at the same time he wondered where she was going.

During a lull in business, Evan walked all around the stand, picking up discarded plastic cups. Scott sat in his chair, jingling the coins in his pocket.

"Man, we are gonna be so rich," said Scott. "I bet we made five bucks already. I bet we made ten! How much you think we made?"

Evan shrugged. He looked at the stack of used cups in his hand and counted the rims. Fourteen. They'd sold fourteen cups so far. And each cup of lemonade cost fifty cents. Evan heard Mrs. DeFazio's voice in his ear. Mrs. DeFazio had been his third-grade teacher, and she'd done everything she could to help Evan with his math.

If one cup of lemonade sells for fifty cents and you sell fourteen cups of lemonade, how much money have you made?

Word problems! Evan hated word problems.

And this one was impossible anyway. He was pretty sure the right equation was

$$14 \times 50 =$$

but how was he supposed to solve that? That was double-digit multiplication. There was no way he could do a problem like that. And besides—some of those fourteen people had bought refills but used the same cup. How many? Evan didn't know.

Still, he knew they'd made a pretty good amount of money. That estimate was close enough for him.

"How much do you think we could make if we sold it *all?*" asked Scott.

"I don't know," said Evan. "Maybe twenty bucks?" That sounded high, even to him, but Evan was an optimist.

"Do you really think?"

Both boys looked in the cooler. Three pitchers were empty. They only had half a pitcher left.

"You were pouring the cups too full," said Scott. "You shoulda poured less in each one."

"You're the one who brought the huge plastic cups. You could fit a gallon in one of those!" said Evan. "Besides, I wasn't gonna be chintzy. They're paying a whole half a buck for it. They deserve a full cup. And anyway, we can just go home and make more. My mom has cans of lemonade in the freezer."

"So go home and make more," said Scott.

"Oh, yes, Your Majesty. O High Commander. Your Infiniteness. Why don't *you* go make it?"

"Cuz I'm chillin'," said Scott, leaning back in his chair with a stupid grin on his face.

Evan knew he was just joking, but this was exactly why he didn't like Scott. He was always thinking of himself. Always looking for some way to come out on top. If they were playing knockout, Scott always came up with a new rule that helped him win. If they were doing an assignment together, Scott always figured out how to divide it so he had less work to do. The kid was a weasel. No two ways about it.

But everyone else was out of town. Evan didn't want to spend the day alone. And Jessie—Jessie was on his "poop list," as Mom called it when the dog did something he wasn't supposed to do. Evan might never play with Jessie again.

Evan crossed the street and went into the house. He was surprised to find that there were no more cans of lemonade in the freezer. Wow. There'd been so many this morning. Luckily there was a can of grape juice in the freezer and a bottle of ginger ale in the fridge. *It'll work,* he thought. *People just want a cold drink. They don't care if it's lemonade.*

He mixed up the grape juice at the sink. The fruit flies were more out of control than ever, thanks to the lemonade the boys had dribbled on the countertop. Evan swatted a couple, but most of them drifted out of his reach and settled on the fruit bowl. He wished his mother believed in chemical warfare. But for Mrs. Treski, it was all-natural or nothing. Usually nothing.

When he went back outside to the lemonade stand, Evan noticed that the last pitcher was turned upside down on the cooler.

"Aw, c'mon, Scott," he said.

"What? It was hot! And you said we could always make more."

"Yeah, well, we didn't have as much in the house as I thought. I've got grape juice and ginger ale."

"I hate ginger ale," Scott said. "I wouldn't give you a penny for it."

It turned out that a lot of people felt the same way. Business was definitely slower. The day got hotter. The sun beat down on them so ferociously that it was easy to imagine the sidewalk cracking open and swallowing them whole.

Fanning himself, Evan asked, "How much money do you really think we could make?"

"I dunno," said Scott, pushing his baseball cap down over his eyes.

"I mean, on a hot day like this," Evan said, silently adding the words *or tomorrow*. "If we sold eight pitchers of lemonade. Whaddya think we'd each make?"

"Eight pitchers? I don't know." Scott shook his head. His baseball-capped face wagged back and forth. "Too hot for math. And it's summer."

Evan pulled the red pen out of his pocket and started to write on the palm of his hand.

$$8 \times ?$$
$$8 \times 50? \quad \div 2?$$

That didn't seem right.

Jessie would know. She'd do that math in a second.

Evan capped the pen and jammed it into his pocket. "But I bet it's a lot," said Evan. "I bet on a hot day like this, we could actually make some real money in the lemonade business."

"Yeah," said Scott. "Then we'd be rich. And I'd get an Xbox. The new one. With the dual controls."

"I'd get an iPod," said Evan. He'd been saving for one for over a year. But every time he had some money put away, well, it just disappeared. Like the ten dollars from Grandma. She'd even written in her card, "Here's a little something to help you get that music thing you want." But the money was gone. He'd treated Paul and Ryan to slices of pizza at Town House. It had been fun.

"That would be so great, to listen to music

whenever I want," said Evan. *I could tune you out,* he added in his own head.

They sat in silence, feeling the heat suck away every bit of their energy. Evan was hatching a plan. The heat wave was supposed to last at least five days. If he and a friend (*not Scott*) set up a lemonade stand every day for five days, he'd definitely have enough to buy an iPod. He imagined himself wearing it as he walked to school. Wearing it on the playground. *Hey, Megan. Yeah, it's my iPod. Sweet, huh?* Wearing it in class when the teacher droned on about fractions and percents. *Nah.* But it would be so cool. At least there would be one thing, *one thing,* that didn't totally stink about going back to school.

After two hours they decided to call it quits. Sales had dropped off—fast—and then stopped altogether.

"Hey, did you notice something?" asked Evan, stacking the chairs.

"What?" said Scott.

"When we started the stand, most of our business came from that direction." He pointed down the street toward the curve in the road. "But after an hour, not one person who walked past us from that direction bought a cup. Not one. They all said, 'No, thanks,' and kept on walking. Why do you think?"

"Dunno," said Scott.

"Boy, you're a real go-getter," said Evan. "You know that?"

Scott socked him in the chest, but Evan defended and knocked Scott's cap off. While Scott was scrambling for his hat, Evan said, "Just hang here for a minute, okay?" and set off down the street. As soon as he rounded the curve, he knew why business had fallen off so badly.

There was Jessie. And *Megan Moriarty* from his class. They were standing inside a wooden booth, and their sign said it all.

LEMONADE
frosty! delicious!
thirst-quenching!
Wow! Only 50 ¢ per cup!

By the looks of it, their business was booming.

Evan watched as Jessie accepted a fistful of dollar bills from a mother surrounded by kids. At that moment, Jessie looked up and saw him. Evan had a weird feeling, like he'd been caught cheating on a test. He wanted to run and hide somewhere. Instead, he froze. What would Jessie do?

Evan couldn't believe it: She sneered at him. She cocked her head to the side and gave him this little I'm-so-much-better-than-you smile. And then—and *then*—she waved the money in her hand at him. She *waved* it! As if to say, "Look how much *we've* made selling lemonade! Bet you can't beat that!"

Evan turned on his heel and walked away. Behind him, he could hear Megan Moriarty laughing at him, clear as a bell.

Chapter 4
Partnership

partnership (pärt′nər-shǐp′) n. Two or more people pooling their money, skills, and resources to run a business, agreeing to share the profits and losses of that business.

Jessie had been waiting for this moment—the moment when Evan would see their lemonade stand, see the wonderful decorations they had made, see the crowds of people waiting in line, see *Megan Moriarty* standing by her side. He would see it all and be so impressed. He would think to himself, *Wow, Jessie is one cool kid. She sure knows how to run a lemonade stand right!* And then he'd jog over and say, "Hey, can I help out?" And Jessie would say, "Sure!

We were hoping you'd come over."

And it would be like old times.

Why hadn't it worked out like that?

With one part of her brain, Jessie continued to take money from customers and make change. That was the part of her brain that worked just fine. With the other part of her brain, Jessie went over what had happened with Evan. That was the part of her brain that tended to run in circles.

She and Megan were selling lemonade. Business had been good. Then Mrs. Pawley, a neighborhood mom, walked up. She had had a bunch of kids in her backyard running through the sprinkler, and now they wanted twelve cups of lemonade. Twelve! It was the biggest sale of the day. Megan got cracking pouring the lemonade and Jessie took the six singles that Mrs. Pawley handed her. All the kids from Mrs. Pawley's backyard were chanting, "Lemon-ADE! Lemon-ADE! Lemon-ADE!"

A fly buzzed by Jessie's ear—they'd been having a problem with flies because of the sticky lemonade spills on their stand—and she cocked her head to one side to shoo it since her hands were busy with the money. And that's when Jessie looked up and saw Evan standing there, staring.

So she smiled.

But he didn't smile back.

So she waved, even though she had all that money in both hands. She waved so he'd know that she was happy to see him.

And then he stalked off, all stiff-legged and bristly. And she never got to say, "Sure! We were hoping you'd come over," like she'd rehearsed in her head.

And just then, Tommy Pawley, who was two years old, pulled down his bathing suit and peed right on the lawn. And Megan laughed so loud, Jessie was sure you could hear it all over the neighborhood.

That's what had happened. That's exactly what had happened. But Jessie knew that something else entirely had happened. And she didn't get it. The way she didn't get a lot of things about people.

All she knew was that the sight of Evan walking

away—walking away from her for the second time that day—made her feel so sad and alone that she just wanted to run home to her room and curl up on her bed with *Charlotte's Web*.

"Hey, Madam Cash Register," said Megan, nudging her. "You're falling behind. Ring three for this lady and one for this kid here."

Jessie turned away from the retreating figure of Evan. "That's a dollar fifty," she said to the woman standing in front of her. She took the five-dollar bill the woman was holding out and made change from her lock box, focusing all her energy on the part of her brain that worked just fine.

It's true that when Evan had first walked out of the garage, Jessie had banged up to her room and tried to think of every way possible that she could make his life a living misery.

She'd thought of telling Mom that Evan was the one who broke the toaster (by playing hockey in the house, which is not allowed). She'd thought of taking back every one of her CDs from his room (even though she knew that would mean she'd have to give back all of *his* CDs). She'd even thought of putting peanut butter in his shoes. (This was something she'd read in a book, and she loved to imagine that moment of horror when he'd think he'd somehow gotten dog doo *inside* his shoes.)

But when these ideas had finished bouncing around her brain, and when her breathing had returned to normal and her fists weren't clenched at her sides anymore, she knew that what she really wanted was to get the old Evan back. The one who was so much fun to be around. The one who helped her out of every jam.

Like when she ate all the Lorna Doones that Mom had set aside for the Girl Scout meeting. And Evan had ridden his bike to the 7-Eleven and bought a new package before Mom even noticed. Or when she accidentally—well, not accidentally, but how was she supposed to know?—picked the red flowers in Grandma's garden that were a hybrid experiment. Evan had said they'd both done it so that Grandma's disappointment was spread around.

Or the time that Jessie had smashed the ceramic heart that Daddy had given her because she was so mad that he had left them. And then, when she had cried about her broken heart, Evan had glued every single last piece back together again.

She wanted back the Evan who was her best friend.

But Evan didn't want *her*, because he thought she was a baby and she was going to embarrass him in Mrs. Overton's class. So she had to prove to him that she was a big kid. That she could keep up with the crowd. That she could fit in—even with his fourth-grade class.

I'll show him I can sell lemonade, too. Just as good as him and Scott. I won't *embarrass him.* So Jessie got down to business.

She knew she needed a partner. From past experience, she'd learned that having a lemonade stand alone wasn't considered cool—it was considered pathetic. And her partner would have to be a fourth-grade girl, because that's what this was all about—showing she could fit in with the fourth-graders. So the question was *who?*

It had to be a girl who lived in the neighborhood, or at least close enough to bike to her house. And it had to be someone that Jessie had talked to at least once. No way could she call up a girl she'd never even talked to. And it had to be someone who seemed nice.

This last part was a problem, because Jessie knew that she often thought people were nice and then they turned out to be not nice. Case in point: those second-grade girls. So Jessie decided it had to be someone who *Evan* thought was nice. Evan knew about these things. He was the one who had explained, with his big arm around her shoulder, "Jessie, those girls are making fun of you. They are *not* nice."

When Jessie thought about all these different requirements, there was only one obvious answer: Megan Moriarty. She lived less than three blocks down the street. Jessie had said hi to her a few times while biking in the neighborhood. And Evan must have thought she was nice because Jessie had found a piece of paper in his trash can with Megan's name written all over it. Why would he cover a page with her name if he didn't think she was a nice person?

Jessie went to the kitchen and climbed onto a stool so that she could reach the cabinet over the stove. She took down the school phone book and looked through the listings for both of last year's third-grade classes. No Megan Moriarty. *Duh,* Jessie remembered—she'd moved in halfway through the school year. With a sinking heart, Jessie checked the town phone book. No Moriarty family listed on Damon Road.

"Okay," said Jessie, slapping the phone book shut and putting it back in the cabinet over the stove. "Time for Plan B."

Jessie went to the hall closet and got out her backpack, which had been hanging there, empty, since the last day of school. Inside she put three cans of frozen lemonade from the freezer and her lock box full of change. (She put the ten-dollar bill, still paper-clipped to last year's birthday card from her grandmother, in her top desk drawer.) Then she went to the garage, strapped on her helmet, and rode off on her bike. As she left the driveway, she could see Evan and Scott's lemonade stand on the corner, but she was careful not to make eye contact. She didn't want to talk to Evan until she was ready to (*ta-da!*) impress him. Her heart leaped when she imagined him ditching Scott to be with her.

Megan's house was so close that Jessie got there in less than thirty seconds. And less than thirty seconds wasn't *nearly* long enough for her to plan what she was going to say. So she rode back and forth in front of the house about fifteen times, trying to pick the right words.

"What're you doing?" a voice shouted from the upstairs window.

Jessie slammed on her foot brakes and looked up. Megan was staring down at her. She looked huge. Her voice did not sound nice.

"Riding my bike," said Jessie.

"But why are you riding back and forth?" asked Megan impatiently. "In front of my house?"

"I dunno," said Jessie. "Ya wanna play?"

"Who are you?" asked Megan.

"Jessie," said Jessie, pointing down the street toward her house.

"Evan's little sister?" asked Megan.

Jessie felt like a deflating balloon. "Yeah."

"Oh," said Megan. "I couldn't tell 'cause of the helmet."

Jessie took her helmet off. "So ya wanna?" she asked.

There was a long pause.

"Where's Evan?" asked Megan.

"He's out, somewhere, with a friend," said Jessie.

"Oh," said Megan. Jessie looked down at the ground.

People tell you things, Evan had told her once, *with their hands and their faces and the way they stand. It's not just what they say. You gotta pay attention, Jess. You gotta watch for the things they're saying, not with their words.*

Jessie looked back up. It was hard to see Megan at all, she was so far up and behind the window screen. Jessie sucked in her breath. "Do you want to do something?"

Another long pause. Jessie started counting in

her head. *One one thousand, two one thousand, three one thousand, four one thousand, five one thousand, six one thousand . . .*

"Sure," said Megan. Then her head disappeared from the window.

A minute later Megan was at the front door. "Hey," she said, opening the screen.

Jessie raised her hand in something that was halfway between a wave and a salute as she walked in. Her sweaty bangs stuck to her forehead where the helmet had mashed them down. She was so nervous about saying something stupid, she didn't say anything at all. Megan leaned against the banister of the stairs and crossed her arms.

"So," said Jessie. She stared at Megan, who was fiddling with the seven or eight band bracelets on her arm. Jessie counted two LiveStrongs, one Red Sox World Champs, one March of Dimes, and one Race for the Cure. "What's that one?" she asked, pointing to a band bracelet with tiger stripes.

Megan stretched it off her wrist and gave it to Jessie. "It's for the Animal Rescue League. My mom gave them some money, so they gave us this and a bumper sticker. I've got twenty-two band bracelets."

"Cool," said Jessie, handing the bracelet back. Megan flipped it back on. She continued to play with the bracelets on her arm, running them up and down, up and down.

"So, whaddya wanna do?" asked Megan.

"I don't know," said Jessie. "We could—I don't know. Let me think. We could—have a lemonade stand!"

"Enhh," said Megan, sounding bored.

"Aw, it'll be fun. Come on!"

"We don't have any lemonade," said Megan.

"I've got three cans," said Jessie. She slipped the backpack off her back and dumped out the three cans of frozen lemonade. Her lock box came rattling out, too.

"What's that?" asked Megan.

"My lock box," said Jessie. "We can use it to make change." She felt her face getting red. Maybe fourth-graders weren't supposed to have lock boxes?

"How much money have you got?" asked Megan.

"You mean in change, or all together?"

Megan pointed at the lock box. "How much is in there?"

"Four dollars and forty-two cents. Fourteen quarters, five dimes, three nickels, and twenty-seven pennies." Jessie didn't say anything about the ten dollars she'd left at home.

Both of Megan's eyebrows shot up. "Exactly?" she asked.

What do those eyebrows mean? Jessie wondered in a panic. Why was Megan smiling at her? *Jessie, those girls are making fun of you. They are* not *nice.*

Jessie didn't say anything. She had a sick feeling in her stomach that this was going to turn out badly.

Megan straightened up. "Wow, you're rich," she said. "Wanna go to the 7-Eleven? We could get Slurpees."

"But—" Jessie pointed to the cans of lemonade on the carpeted hallway floor. The frost on them was already starting to sweat off.

"We could do the lemonade stand later," said Megan. "Maybe."

Jessie thought of Scott and Evan, racking up

sales two blocks down. How was she going to prove herself to Evan if she couldn't even get Megan to *have* a stand?

"How about the lemonade stand *first?*" Jessie said. "And then Slurpees with our earnings. I bet we'd even have enough for chips. And gum!"

"You think?" said Megan.

"I *know*," said Jessie. "Look." She held up a can of lemonade. "It says right on the can: 'Yields sixty-four ounces.' So we get eight cups from each can and sell each cup for half a buck, so that's four bucks, and then there're three cans, so that's twelve bucks altogether. Right?" The numbers flashed in Jessie's brain so fast, she didn't even need to think about what she was multiplying and dividing and adding. It just made sense to her.

"Hey, how old are you?" Megan asked, looking at her sideways.

"Eight," said Jessie. "But I'll be nine next month."

Megan shook her head. "That math doesn't sound right. No way we can make twelve dollars from just three little cans."

"Yuh-hunh," said Jessie. "I'll show you. Do you have a piece of paper?"

Jessie started to draw pictures. She knew that other kids couldn't see the numbers the way she did. They needed the pictures to make sense of math.

"Look," she said. "Here are three pitchers of lemonade, 'cause we've got three cans of lemonade. And each pitcher's got sixty-four ounces in it.

"Now, when we pour a cup of lemonade, we'll pour eight ounces, 'cause that's how much a cup holds. You don't want to pour less than that, or people will say you're being a cheapskate. So each pitcher is going to give us eight cups. 'Cause eight times eight equals sixty-four, right?

"Now, we'll sell each cup for fifty cents. That's a fair price. That means that every time we sell *two* cups, we make a buck. Right? Because fifty cents plus fifty cents equals a dollar. So look. I'll circle the cups by twos, and that's how many dollars we make. Count 'em."

Megan counted the circled pairs of cups. ". . . ten, eleven, twelve."

"That's how much money we'll make," said

Jessie. "*If* we sell all the lemonade. And *if* we do the lemonade stand."

"Wow," said Megan. "You're really good at math." She puffed her cheeks out like a bullfrog and thought for a minute. Then she popped both cheeks with her hands and said, "Whatever. Let's do the lemonade thing."

Jessie felt soaked in relief. Maybe this was going to work after all.

An hour later, Jessie and Megan had transformed the little wooden puppet theater in Megan's basement into the hottest new lemonade stand on the block. The stand was decorated with tissue-paper flowers, cut-out butterflies, and glittery hearts. It was a showstopper.

And, boy, did people notice it. Kids in the neighborhood, strangers walking their dogs, moms strolling with carriages—even the two guys fixing the telephone wires. They all came to buy lemonade. And just when Jessie and Megan were on the verge of running out, Mrs. Moriarty went to the store and bought three more cans—free of charge!

So when Mrs. Pawley asked for twelve cups at exactly the moment that Evan rounded the curve and saw her lemonade stand, Jessie felt like she'd just scored a hundred on a test *and* gotten five points for extra credit.

So why did Evan stomp off?

And how come she didn't feel like she'd won anything at all?

Chapter 5
competition

competition (kŏm′pĭ-tĭsh′ən) n. Rivalry in the marketplace.

Dinner that night at the Treskis' was quiet. So the explosion that followed seemed *especially* loud.

It was Jessie's turn to clear and scrape the dishes, Evan's turn to wash and stack. Evan looked at the pile of dirty plates on his left. Jessie was ahead. She was always ahead when it was her turn to clear, but tonight it felt like she was taunting him. To Evan, every plate-scraping sounded like "Can't keep up. Can't keep up."

Evan was scrubbing the casserole pan when

Jessie stacked the last dirty dish by his elbow. Then she stuck her hands under the faucet to rinse without even saying excuse me and shook her hands *practically right in Evan's face* and said, "So how much money did you make?"

That was it! He couldn't hold it in any longer!

"Why'd you do it, huh? Why'd you have to ruin the one thing I had going?" For a second, Evan wasn't sure if he meant the lemonade stand or Megan Moriarty. In a mixed-up way, he meant both.

And there was *no way* he was going to tell Jessie that after paying back his mother for the four cans of lemonade, one can of grape juice, and one bottle of ginger ale (she'd been pretty irritated when she came down from the office and there wasn't a single cold drink in the house), he had walked away with two dollars and eleven cents. On top of that, he was pretty sure Scott had kept the five-dollar bill they'd earned. Well, what was Evan supposed to do? Ask Scott to turn his pockets inside out? Evan hadn't kept track of the sales, so he couldn't be sure.

"Why'd *I* do it? Why'd *you* do it? Why'd you invite that *jerk* over for a lemonade stand?" shouted Jessie. "And how come you wouldn't let me play? You're the one who was mean."

"You're such a showoff," said Evan. "You always have to let everyone know that you're the smart one."

"I wasn't showing off. I was just trying to have a little fun. Is that against the law? You won't do a lemonade stand with me. Then I won't do a lemonade stand with you. I'll do one with my friend Megan, instead."

"You can-*not* be her friend. You can-*not* be her friend!" shouted Evan.

"Why not?"

"Because you're a little kid. You don't even belong in the fourth grade. And because you're just an annoying showoff pest and no one likes you!"

The words felt like disgusting spiders running out of his mouth. They were horrible. But it felt so *good* to get rid of them.

Then Evan saw Jessie's lip tremble. Uh-oh. Jessie was a howler. She didn't cry often and she didn't cry

61

long. But when she did, it was loud. Mom would come down from her office. Evan would catch the blame. *Unfair*.

But Jessie didn't let loose. Instead, she stood as tall as her runty height would allow and said, "Megan likes me. She invited me over to her house tomorrow. We're going to make another lemonade stand and earn *twice* what we did today."

Oh, that was *it*! She was going to ruin everything. Show him up right in front of Megan. Even before the school year started! Make Megan think he was just some stupid loser who couldn't even beat out his baby sister at a lemonade stand. Evan boiled over.

"I wouldn't count on it, *Juicy*," he said. Jessie hated that nickname, and Evan only used it when he had to. "I'm going to have a lemonade stand every day until school starts. And I'm going to earn a hundred bucks by the end of the summer. Enough for an iPod."

"Oh, *please*. Like you *could* if you even wanted to," said Jessie. "Megan and I already made twelve bucks each today. We could have a hundred dollars like *that*." Jessie snapped her fingers.

"And then what?" said Evan. "You'd lock it up in your lock box and save it 'til you were fifty years old. You're the biggest miser on this planet."

Jessie stiffened up. Her mouth made a funny O. But then she put a hand on her hip and smirked at Evan. "For your information, I'm going to make a one-hundred-dollar donation to a *charity*."

Evan snorted. "Yeah, right. What charity?"

There was a long pause. And then Jessie said, as smooth as whipped cream, "The Animal Rescue League. Megan and I talked about it today."

"You don't even like animals," said Evan.

"Everybody likes animals!" shouted Jessie. "And I'm going to give them a hundred dollars. So you can't *ever* call me a miser again."

"I hope I never have to *talk* to you again," shouted Evan.

"Hey!" a sharp voice called from the stairs. Mrs. Treski had a pencil stuck in her hair and a worried look on her face. "I could hear you two all the way in the attic. With the air conditioner on high. What's up?"

Evan looked at Jessie. Jessie looked at Evan.

They had taken a vow. A spit vow.

Ever since Dad had gone, they had vowed not to fight in front of Mom. It made her sad. Sadder, even, than when Dad left.

"Nothing," said Evan.

"Nothing," said Jessie.

Mrs. Treski looked at the two of them. "Come on. Out with it. What are you two yelling about?"

"It wasn't a fight, Mom," said Evan. "We were just joking around."

"Yeah," said Jessie. "We were goofing. Sorry we got you out of your office."

Mrs. Treski looked at both of them with her laser eyes. Jessie hung the dishtowel on the oven handle and fiddled with it until it was perfectly straight. Evan bent over the casserole pan and scrubbed as if his life depended on it. He scrubbed so hard, his elbow bumped the fruit bowl. A cloud of fruit flies rose into the air and then settled back down.

"Oh, God," said Mrs. Treski. "Would you look at those fruit flies!" Her shoulders slumped. "All right. Well, I'm going back up. Can you guys handle showers and reading, and then I'll be down to tuck and turn off lights?"

"Sure, Mom," said Jessie.

"No problem," said Evan.

Mrs. Treski disappeared upstairs. Jessie turned to Evan at the sink.

"Let's make a bet," she said. "Whoever earns a hundred dollars wins. And the *loser* has to give all their earnings to the winner."

Evan shook his head. "Not fair," he said. "You've already got money saved up."

"That money doesn't count," said Jessie. "We'll start with today's earnings. And it's *all* got to be from selling lemonade. No mowing lawns or sweeping out the garage or anything else."

"Aw, what if neither one of us makes a hundred?" said Evan, not liking the sound of this deal.

"Then whoever makes the closest to a hundred wins. And even if we *both* make over a hundred, whoever makes the most money wins the bet."

"When do we count up the money?" asked Evan.

Jessie thought about that. "Sunday night. Right before the fireworks." She looked straight at Evan. "Huh? Whaddya say?"

Evan didn't like bets. He really wasn't that into competition. He loved to play basketball and always gave it his all. But winning or losing—it didn't make much difference to him. He just liked to play.

But this. This was different. This mattered. If he didn't beat Jessie at this bet, if he couldn't win against his little sister in a lemonade war, then— Evan thought of the school year stretching in front of him—it was all over. He might as well just give up on everything right now.

"It's a bet. A hundred bucks by Sunday night. Winner takes all." He shook his wet hands over the sink, dried them on the dishtowel, and gave Jessie his most menacing look. "You better pray for mercy."

Chapter 6
underselling

underselling (un'dər-sĕl'ĭng) v. Pricing the same goods for less than the competition.

Jessie knew that Evan was up to something. First of all, there were all those phone calls last night. At least ten of them.

Then, he'd come knocking on her door this morning, asking if he could have the pieces of foam core she had leaning against her bedroom wall.

"No way," she'd answered. "That's for my Labor Day display."

"Oh, give it up. Today's Thursday. The contest is on Monday, and you don't even have an idea," Evan said.

"I do too have an idea. I'm just not telling *you*." Jessie still didn't have a clue about her Labor Day project, but she wasn't going to give Evan the satisfaction of knowing that.

"Then how come you haven't done anything?" Evan said, pointing at the blank foam core and the bags of untouched art supplies. "You're supposed to have pictures and typed-up information and a big title. It's supposed to be like a school report."

Jessie scrunched her eyes and pursed her lips in a you're-such-an-idiot look. "Don't worry. It's going to be great, and it's going to win first prize. And anyway, Mom bought all those supplies for *me,* and I'm not giving anything to *you*."

Jessie heard Evan mutter, "Miser," just as she slammed the door in his face.

And now three of Evan's friends were over— Paul, Jack, and Ryan. And all three had shown up with paper bags. And they were all in the garage making a lot of noise, with a big KEEP OUT sign taped to the door. Not that Jessie would have gone in there anyway. Who cares what a bunch of boys are doing? But she wished Megan had invited her to come over before lunch instead of after.

Jessie went into the kitchen to make a turkey sandwich. The boys had left a slimy mess of peanut butter, Doritos, and—yes—sticky puddles of lemonade mix. Jessie quickly looked in the trash can under the kitchen sink. There were twelve empty cans of frozen lemonade mix. Twelve! That was ninety-six cups' worth of lemonade. Ninety-six possible sales. Holy cow!

Where had Evan gotten the lemonade? He hadn't gone to the store, and he didn't have any money anyway. Then Jessie remembered the paper bags that Paul, Ryan, and Jack had carried in. She bet the boys had all raided their freezers and brought over a stash.

That didn't seem fair! She and Megan had to buy their lemonade today, using the money they'd made yesterday. How were they going to stay ahead of the game if the boys had free lemonade to sell?

"Think, Jessie, think," she whispered to herself. She couldn't let those boys win.

By the time she finished her lunch and cleaned up her mess (she wasn't going to lift a *finger* to clean up the boys' mess), she had the beginning of a plan in her head.

Which is why she found it doubly confusing when she knocked on Megan's screen and Carly Brownell came to the door. Jessie'd been all ready to say, "I've got a great idea." But then there was Carly, looking down at her like she was an earwig.

"Um, is Megan home?" asked Jessie.

Carly didn't open the screen door as she looked left and right behind Jessie. "Where's Evan?"

"Huh?" said Jessie.

Megan came running down the stairs carrying bottles of nail polish. "Oh, hi, Jessie," she said, opening the door. She poked her head out and looked around. "Where's Evan?"

"He's at home. Why?" asked Jessie. Carly made a noise like a snorting hippopotamus.

"I thought you said he was coming," said Megan.

"No, I didn't," said Jessie. "You said it would be fun to make a lemonade stand with all three of us, and I said, yeah, that would be fun."

"So, didn't he want to?" asked Megan.

"I never asked him," said Jessie.

"Oh. I thought you were going to," said Megan.

"Then you should have said, 'Hey, Jessie. Ask Evan if he wants to make a lemonade stand tomorrow.' And then I would have asked him." This was exactly what drove Jessie crazy about girls. They always said things halfway and then expected you to get the other half. And Jessie never got the other half.

Carly gave Megan a look. Jessie wasn't positive what the look meant, but she was pretty sure it wasn't a nice one.

That was the other thing that Jessie hated about girls. They were always giving looks. Looks that contained all kinds of strange and complicated messages.

Last year, in second grade, there had been four girls who were always exchanging looks with one another—Becky Baker, Lorelei Sun, Andrea Hennessey, and Eileen Garrett. Jessie watched them and knew that Evan was right: They talked without words. They used their eyes to pass secret messages. She also knew they didn't like her, but only because Evan had finally explained it to her over Christmas vacation. Jessie was surprised when he told her this. They laughed so much—how could they be mean?

They were the four who started the club: the Wild Hot Jellybeans Club. Or, as they called it, the WHJ Club. Becky was president, and she was always telling the others what to do. They made signs and paper buttons and membership cards. The teacher, Mrs. Soren, didn't usually allow clubs in the classroom, but she made an exception, telling the girls, "I'll let you wear your buttons in class, but only if you let all the other kids join—if they want to." By the end of the day, every kid in class was wearing a WHJ button—even Jessie, who'd never belonged to a club before.

It had seemed like Becky was being so nice to her. "That should have been your first clue," Evan told Jessie later. Becky made extra buttons for Jessie and even helped tape them all over her shirt. And she made a special membership card for her and even a

WHJ sign that she helped Jessie glue onto her Writers' Workshop folder.

Jessie remembered all the girls laughing and Jessie laughing, too. And all those strange looks that Becky and Lorelei and Andrea and Eileen kept flashing back and forth, like secret notes passed in class that Jessie could never read.

The very next day, Mrs. Soren collected all the buttons, gathered up all the membership cards, and even replaced Jessie's Writers' Workshop folder. "No clubs in the classroom," she said. "I made a bad choice by allowing it, even for one day."

On the playground, Jessie went up to Becky. "Why is she breaking up the club?" she asked.

Becky gave her a sour look. She'd been grumpy all morning. "Don't you get it, you dummy? WHJ doesn't stand for Wild Hot Jellybeans. We just said that to Mrs. Soren. It stands for We Hate Jessie. It's the We Hate Jessie Club, and everyone in the class is a member."

Jessie stared at Becky. Why did they hate her? What had she ever done to them? It didn't make sense. And then Lorelei, Andrea, and Eileen had laughed, and even Becky had managed a smirky grin.

"Jerks," Evan said later, when Jessie told him the whole story. "They've got rocks for brains. But Jess, you gotta be on the lookout for girls like that."

Standing in Megan's front hall, Jessie stared at Carly. Something inside told her Carly was a "girl like that."

"Look," said Jessie. "It doesn't matter. Evan can't come over. He's busy. And we've got to get going on our lemonade stand. I've got a great idea."

"We don't want to do a lemonade stand," said Carly.

Jessie looked at Megan.

"It's just that . . ." Megan fiddled with the bottles of nail polish in her hand the same way she'd fiddled with her band bracelets the day before. "It's kind of hot. And we did the lemonade thing already. And now Carly is over. So. Ya know?"

"You said you wanted to," said Jessie. *And I thought you liked me,* she added in her head. She felt her lower lip tremble. *Not now,* she shouted inside. *Don't you be a big baby!*

Megan stood there, saying nothing, fiddling with the bottles. Then she turned to Carly. "Aw, c'mon, Carly. It'll be fun. We made a *ton* of money yesterday. And it was really . . . fun."

Carly crossed her arms, tightened her lips, and raised one eyebrow. It was amazing how high she could raise that eyebrow. Jessie had never seen an eyebrow go that high.

"Aw, c'mon, Carly," Megan said again. Carly didn't move a muscle.

"Well, then I guess . . . " Megan's voice trailed off. She clicked one bottle of nail polish against another so that it made a tapping sound that filled the long silence. "I guess me and Jessie will do the lemonade stand alone then."

Carly dropped her eyebrow and her arms. "What-*ever*," she said as she walked out the door. "Spend the day baby-sitting if you want." The screen door slammed, followed by a huge bucketful of silence.

"What-*ever*," said Megan, imitating Carly's voice.

Jessie laughed, even though she was still stinging from the baby-sitting remark. "Thanks for doing the lemonade stand with me," she said.

"Are you kidding?" said Megan. "She's such a stuck-up jerk. I didn't even invite her over. She just rode by, and when I said that you and Evan might be coming over, she just walked into the house."

"Are all the girls in fourth grade like her?" asked Jessie. She tried to sound casual.

"Some are, some aren't," said Megan. She sat down on the stairs and opened a bottle of sky blue nail polish. With quick expert strokes, she started painting her toenails. "Hey, that's right. You're going to be in our class this year. That's so weird. Jumping a grade."

"A lot of people skip a grade," said Jessie.

"Really? I never met one before. Here. Do your toes green and then we'll be coordinated."

Jessie ended up getting more polish on her toes than on her toenails. But by the time they were done, Jessie had explained her plan for the day: Value-added.

"See," she said, pulling *Ten Bright Ideas to Light Up Your Sales* from the back pocket of her shorts. She turned to Bright Idea #2 and pointed with her finger.

> VALUE-ADDED: SOMETHING EXTRA (SUCH AS A SPECIAL FEATURE OR ATTRACTIVE PACKAGING) ADDED BY A COMPANY TO A PRODUCT THAT MAKES THE PRODUCT MORE DESIRABLE IN THE MARKETPLACE.

"That means we give customers something extra they didn't expect," explained Jessie. "I mean, anyone can go home and mix up their own batch of lemonade. Right? So if we want them to buy from us, we've got to give them something extra. We *add value*."

"Great," said Megan. "What are we going to add?"

"Well, how about chips? And maybe pretzels. Everyone likes chips and pretzels. We'll just have a bowl on the table, and anyone who buys lemonade can have some free snacks."

"So we're adding value—snacks."

"Yeah, except—" Jessie had stayed up late last night reading her mom's booklet. "You know what we're really adding? Fun. That's the one thing people can't get all by themselves. It *looks* like we're selling lemonade and snacks. But we're really selling fun. And everyone wants fun."

"Wow," said Megan. "That's really smart. It'll be like a party. Who doesn't like a party?"

Jessie nodded her head. She carefully tore out the definition of *value-added* from the booklet and put it in her lock box. Her mother always said: *Some ideas are like money in the bank.*

An hour later, they were all set up. The lemonade stand was newly decorated with streamers and balloons. Three bowls of snacks—Cheetos, potato chips, and pretzels—were set on top. Jessie had lugged Megan's boom box all the way downstairs, and Megan was doing the DJ thing with her CD collection. It looked like a party had somehow sprung up right in the middle of the hot concrete sidewalk. To anyone passing by, the lemonade stand shouted out, "Come over here! This is where the fun is!"

As soon as the music had come on, customers

had started drifting over. One of the moms across the street set up a sprinkler in her front yard, and soon all the kids in the neighborhood were running through the sprinkler and grabbing handfuls of Cheetos. Two women walking their dogs stopped for a nibble and ended up staying an hour. And three or four of the neighborhood mothers set up lawn chairs nearby and talked and ate pretzels while their kids ran through the water.

But Jessie noticed a funny thing. Even though there was an endless buzz of activity around the stand and the chips were flying out of the bowls faster than Megan could restock them, they weren't selling much lemonade.

"Hey, Jordan," said Jessie, as a four-year-old boy ran by in a bathing suit. "Don't you want a cup of lemonade?"

Jordan dive-bombed the pretzel bowl and came up with a fistful. "I had too much already. Four glasses!" and off he ran.

"Four glasses!" said Jessie to Megan. "He didn't buy any! Mrs. Doran, don't you want a cup of lemonade?"

"Sorry, Jessie, I have to pass," said Mrs. Doran. "I had two already, and I'm trying to cut down on sugary drinks."

Where's everybody drinking so much lemonade? wondered Jessie. She looked down the road. *Oh, wait a minute.* "Megan, hold down the fort," said Jessie. "I'll be right back."

"Sure thing," said Megan, dancing to the music. "This lemonade stand was the greatest idea. It's like a birthday for the whole neighborhood!"

Jessie headed down the road. As she rounded the bend, she prepared for the worst: Evan's lemonade stand crowded with customers. But there was nothing. Absolutely nothing. The corner was deserted.

She crossed the street and went into the garage. There was the cooler, dirty and empty. And there were the stacked plastic chairs, four of them this time. And there was—wait a minute. Those were *new* signs.

Jessie pulled out three large pieces of foam core. On the back of each one was part of the penguin project Evan had done last year in third grade. On the front were big letters:

Slow down!
Cheapest lemonade in town!
Ahead!

Yesterday's prices!
Today's lemonade!

You won't believe your eyes!
Icy cold lemonade!
Just 10¢ a cup!

Jessie *couldn't* believe her eyes. *Ten* cents a cup. That was crazy! Even if they sold all ninety-six cups, they'd only make $9.60. And split four ways—that was just $2.40 for each boy. Evan was never going to earn a hundred dollars with that kind of profit.

Jessie went down into the basement. Evan and Paul were playing air hockey. *Whashoo*. The puck flew into Evan's goal and Paul threw his arms into the air in a victory V.

"Oh, snap!" said Evan. "You're winning."

"Winning? Winning? Are you kidding me?" said Paul. Then he dropped his voice to a gravelly growl and said, "I don't play to win. I play to *pul-ver-ize*." Just like that muscle-guy actor in *Agent Down*, the movie that all the boys were talking about. Paul was even flexing his muscles like that actor—except that Paul didn't have any muscles. At least none that Jessie could see.

When Paul saw Jessie, he dropped his arms. "Hey," he said. Paul was Jessie's favorite of Evan's friends. He always joked around with her, but in a nice way. And he never minded when Evan invited her to come along with them.

"Hey," said Jessie. "What's up?"

Evan turned off the air hockey table. "Nothing," he said. "We were just going out."

Paul dropped his hockey paddle onto the table and followed Evan into the garage. Jessie trailed behind.

"Where are you going?" she asked.

"Down to the tracks," said Paul as he strapped on his bike helmet. "We put pennies there this morning, so we're gonna get 'em now. Squash! Ya wanna—"

"YO!" shouted Evan.

"My B," muttered Paul. "So, see ya," he said to Jessie.

Jessie hated this feeling of being shut out. Like she wasn't wanted. Evan had never made her feel that way before, even when sometimes he *did* want to be just with his friends. He'd always say things like, "Jess, we're going to go shoot hoops just the two of us, but when we get back we'll play spud with you." So that she knew he still liked her, even when she wasn't invited along.

But this. This was like he hated her. Like he never wanted to play with her again. And Paul was going right along with it.

Jessie scowled. "So you really cleaned up today at the lemonade stand, huh?" she said.

"Yep, we sold out," said Evan.

"So what did you make, like three dollars?" she asked.

"Actually, we made a ton. What was it, Paul?"

"Forty-five bucks," said Paul.

Jessie's mouth went slack. Forty-five dollars! "There's no way," she said. "Not at ten cents a cup."

"Oh, just the little kids paid that," said Evan. "The grownups all gave us way more. 'That's too cheap!' they said. 'It's such a hot day and you're working so hard. Here, take a dollar. Keep the change.' It was crazy!"

"Unreal," said Paul. "They kept pushing all this money at us 'cause they thought it was so sweet we were selling lemonade for a dime. We made a killing."

Bright Idea #5—Jessie remembered it immediately. "That's called *goodwill*," she said slowly, picturing the exact page from her mother's booklet with the definition on it.

GOODWILL: AN INTANGIBLE BUT RECOGNIZED ASSET THAT RESULTS FROM MAKING/SELLING GOOD PRODUCTS, HAVING GOOD RELATIONSHIPS WITH YOUR CUSTOMERS AND SUPPLIERS, AND BEING WELL REGARDED IN THE COMMUNITY.

"It's when you do something nice in business and it ends up paying you back with money." She sighed. Why hadn't she thought of that? She would be sure to tear out that definition and put it in her lock box when she got back to the lemonade stand.

"Well, whatever. We cleaned up," said Evan.

"Even so," said Jessie, trying to find some way to prove that Evan had *not* had a good day selling lemonade. "You had four people working the stand. So if you split forty-five dollars four ways, that's only eleven twenty-five each." *Which is still way more than I'm going to make today,* she thought, *since the whole neighborhood has already filled up on cheap lemonade.*

"We're not splitting," said Evan. "The guys said I could keep it all."

"Right," said Paul. "All for a good cause!"

"That's not fair!" said Jessie.

"Sure it is," said Evan as he got on his bike and pushed off. "In case you didn't know, that's what it's like to have *friends*." Evan crossed the street.

"Ouch," said Paul. "TTFN, Jess." He followed Evan.

Jessie was left standing alone in the driveway.

Chapter 7
Location, Location, Location

location (lō-kā′shən) n. Real estate term that refers to the position of a piece of real estate as it relates to the value of that real estate.

Evan was in trouble. So far, he'd earned forty-seven dollars and eleven cents, which was more money than he'd ever had in his whole life. But today was Friday. There were only three days left. Three days to beat Jessie. He needed to earn almost fifty-three dollars to win the bet. And that meant each day he had to earn—

Evan tried to do the math in his head. Fifty-three divided by three. Fifty-three divided by three. His brain spun like a top. He didn't know where to begin.

He went to his desk, pulled out a piece of paper—his basketball schedule from last winter—and flipped it over to the back. He found the stub of a pencil in his bottom desk drawer, and on the paper he wrote

$$53 \div 3 =$$

He stared and stared at the equation on the page. The number fifty-three was just too big. He didn't know how to do it.

"Jessie would know how," he muttered, scribbling hard on the page. Jessie could do long division. Jessie had her multiplication facts memorized all the way up to fourteen times fourteen. Jessie would look at a problem like this and just do it in her head. *Snap.*

Evan felt his mouth getting tight, his fingers gripping the pencil too hard, as he scribbled a dark storm cloud on the page. His math papers from school were always covered in *X*'s. Nobody else got as many *X*'s as he did. Nobody.

Draw a picture. Mrs. DeFazio's voice floated in his head. She had always reminded him to draw a picture when he couldn't figure out how to start a math problem. *A picture of what?* he asked in his head. *Anything,* came the answer.

Anything? Yes, anything, as long as there are fifty-three of them.

Dollar signs. Evan decided to draw dollar signs.

He started to draw three rows of dollar signs.

"One, two, three," he counted, as he drew:

$

$

$

"Four, five, six." He drew:

$ $

$ $

$ $

By the time he reached fifty-three, his page looked like this:

$ $ $ $ $ $ $ $ $ $ $ $ $ $ $ $ $ $ $

$ $ $ $ $ $ $ $ $ $ $ $ $ $ $ $ $ $ $

$ $ $ $ $ $ $ $ $ $ $ $ $ $ $ $ $

There were seventeen dollar signs in each row. And then those two extra dollar signs left over. Evan drew a ring around those two extras.

$ $ $ $ $ $ $ $ $ $ $ $ $ $ $ $$ ⟮$⟯

$ $ $ $ $ $ $ $ $ $ $ $ $ $ $ $ $⟮$⟯

$ $ $ $ $ $ $ $ $ $ $ $ $ $ $ $ $

Seventeen dollar signs. And two left over. Evan stared at the picture for a long time. He wrote "Friday" next to the first row, "Saturday" next to the second row, and "Sunday" next to the third row.

Friday $ $ $ $ $ $ $ $ $ $ $ $ $ $ $ $ $ ($)

Saturday $ $ $ $ $ $ $ $ $ $ $ $ $ $ $ $ $ ($)

Sunday $ $ $ $ $ $ $ $ $ $ $ $ $ $ $ $ $

Evan looked at the picture. It started to make sense. He needed to make seventeen dollars on Friday, seventeen dollars on Saturday, and seventeen dollars on Sunday. And somewhere over the three days, he needed to make two *extra* bucks in order to earn fifty-three dollars by Sunday evening.

Evan felt his heart jump in his chest. He had done it. He had figured out fifty-three divided by three. That was a *fourth-grade* problem. That was *fourth-grade* math. And he hadn't even started fourth grade! And no one had helped him. Not Mom, not Grandma, not Jessie. He'd done it all by himself. It was like shooting the winning basket in double overtime! He hadn't felt this good since the Lemonade War had begun.

But seventeen dollars a day? How was he going to do that? Yesterday he'd made forty-five dollars, but that was because he'd had help (and free supplies) from his friends. They weren't going to want to run a lemonade stand every day. Especially on the last days of summer vacation.

He needed a plan. Something that would guarantee good sales. The weather was holding out, that was for sure. It was going to hit 95 degrees today. A real scorcher. People would be thirsty, all right. Evan closed his eyes and imagined a crowd of thirsty people, all waving dollar bills at him. Now where was he going to find a lot of thirsty people with money to spend?

An idea popped into Evan's head. *Yep!* It was perfect. He just needed to find something with wheels to get him there.

It took Evan half an hour to drag his loaded wagon to the town center—a distance he usually traveled in less than five minutes by bike. But once he was there, he knew it was worth it.

It was lunchtime and the shaded benches on the town green were filled with people sprawling in the heat. Workers from the nearby stores on their half-hour lunch breaks, moms out with their kids, old people who didn't want to be cooped up in their houses all day. High school kids on skateboards slooshed by. Preschoolers climbed on the life-size sculpture of a circle of children playing ring-around-the-rosey. Dogs lay under trees, their tongues hanging out, *pant, pant, pant.*

Evan surveyed the scene and picked his spot, right in the center of the green where all the paths met. Anyone walking across the green would have to pass his stand. And who could resist lemonade on a day as hot as this?

But first he wheeled his wagon off to the side, parking it halfway under a huge rhododendron. Then he crossed the street and walked into the Big Dipper.

The frozen air felt good on his skin. It was like getting dunked in a vat of just-melted ice cream. And the smells—*mmmmmm*. A mix of vanilla, chocolate, coconut, caramel, and bubblegum. He looked at the tubs of ice cream, all in a row, carefully protected behind a pane of glass. The money in his pocket tingled. He had plenty left over after buying five cans of frozen lemonade mix with his earnings from yesterday. What would it hurt to buy just one cone? Or a milk shake? Or maybe both?

"Can I help you?" asked the woman behind the counter.

"Uh, yeah," said Evan. He stuck his hand in his pocket and felt all the money. Bills and coins ruffled between his fingers. Money was meant to be spent. Why not spend a little?

"I, uh . . ." Evan could just imagine how good the ice cream would feel sliding down his hot throat. Creamy. Sweet. Like cold, golden deliciousness. He let his mind float as he gazed at the swirly buckets of ice cream.

The sound of laughter brought him back to earth in a hurry. He looked around. It was just some girls he didn't know at the water fountain. But it had *sounded* like Megan Moriarty.

"Can you please tell me how much a glass of lemonade costs?"

"Three dollars," said the woman.

"Really?" said Evan. "That much? How big's the cup?"

The woman pulled a plastic cup off a stack and held it up. It wasn't much bigger than the eight-ounce cups Evan had in his wagon.

"Wow. Three bucks. That's a lot," said Evan. "Well, thanks anyway." He started to walk to the door.

"Hey," said the woman, pointing to the ice cream case. "I'm allowed to give you a taste for free."

"Really?" said Evan. "Then, uh, could I taste the Strawberry Slam?" The woman handed him a tiny plastic spoon with three licks' worth of pink ice cream on it. Evan swallowed it all in one gulp. *Aahhh.*

Back outside, he got to work. First he filled his pitchers with water from the drinking fountain. Then he stirred in the mix. Then he pulled out a big blue marker and wrote on a piece of paper, "$2 per cup. Best price in town."

He'd barely finished setting up when the customers started lining up. And they didn't stop. For a full hour, he poured lemonade. *The world is a thirsty place,* he thought as he nearly emptied his fourth pitcher of the day. *And I am the Lemonade King.*

(Later, Evan would think of something his grandma said: "Pride goeth before a fall.")

When Evan looked up, there was Officer Ken, his hands on his hips, looking down on him. Evan gulped. He stared at the large holstered gun strapped to Officer Ken's belt.

"Hello," said Officer Ken, not smiling.

"Hi," said Evan. Officer Ken did the Bike Rodeo every year at Evan's school. He was also the cop who had shown up last fall when there was a hurt goose on the recess field. Officer Ken was always smiling. *Why isn't he smiling now?* Evan wondered.

"Do you have a permit?" asked Officer Ken. He had a very deep voice, even when he talked quietly, like he did now.

"You mean, like, a bike permit?" That's what the Rodeo was all about. If they passed the Rodeo, the third-graders got their bike permits, which meant they were allowed to ride to school.

"No. I mean a permit to sell food and beverages in a public space. You need to get a permit from the town hall. And pay a fee for the privilege."

Pay the town hall to run a lemonade stand? Was he kidding? Evan looked at Officer Ken's face. He didn't look like he was kidding.

"I didn't know I needed one," said Evan.

"Sorry, friend," said Officer Ken. "I'm going to have to shut you down. It's the law."

"But . . . but . . . there are lemonade stands all over town," said Evan. He thought of Jessie and Megan's lemonade stand. When he'd wheeled by with his wagon more than an hour ago, their stand had looked like a beehive, with small kids crowding around. He had read the sign over their stand: FREE FACE-PAINTING! NAIL-POLISHING! HAIR-BRAIDING! What a gimmick! But it sure looked like it was working. "You know," said Evan, "there's a stand on Damon Road right now. You should go bust them."

Officer Ken smiled. "We tend to look the other way when it's in a residential neighborhood. But right here, on the town green, we have to enforce the law. Otherwise we'd have someone selling something every two feet."

"But—" There had to be some way to convince Officer Ken. How could Evan make him understand? "You see, I've got this little sister. And we've got a . . . a . . . competition going. To see who can sell the most lemonade. And I've *got* to win. Because she's . . ." He couldn't explain the rest. About fourth grade. And how embarrassed he was to be in the same class as his kid sister. And how it made him feel like a great big loser.

Evan looked up at Officer Ken. Officer Ken looked down at Evan. It was like Officer Ken was wearing a mask. A no-smiling, I'm-not-your-buddy mask.

Then Officer Ken shook his head and smiled and the mask fell off. "I've got a little sister, too," he said. "Love her to death, *now,* but when we were kids—" Officer Ken sucked in his breath and shook his head again. *"Hooo!"*

Then the mask came back, and Officer Ken looked right at Evan for ten very stern seconds.

"Tell you what," said Officer Ken. "I *do* have to shut you down. The law's the law. But before I do, I'll buy one last glass of lemonade. How's that sound?"

Evan's face fell. "Sure," he said without enthusiasm. He poured an extra-tall cup and gave it to the policeman.

Officer Ken reached into his pocket and handed Evan a five-dollar bill. "Keep the change," he said. "A contribution to the Big Brother Fund. Now clean up your things and don't leave any litter behind." He lifted his cup in a toast as he walked away.

Evan watched him go. *Wow,* he thought. *I just sold the most expensive cup of lemonade in town.*

Evan stared at the five-dollar bill in his hand.

It was funny. Two days ago, he would have felt as rich as a king to have that money in his hands. It was enough to buy two slices of pizza and a soda with his friends. It was enough to rent a video and have a late night at someone's house. It was enough to buy a whole bagful of his favorite candy mix at CVS.

Two days ago, he would have been jumping for joy.

Now he looked at the five dollars and thought, *It's nothing.* Compared to the one hundred dollars he needed to win the war, five dollars was *nothing.* He felt somehow that he'd been robbed of something—maybe the happiness he should have been feeling.

He loaded everything from his stand into the wagon, making sure he didn't leave a scrap of litter behind. He still had a glassful of lemonade left in one pitcher, not to mention another whole pitcher already mixed up and unsold, so he poured himself a full cup. Then, before beginning the long, hot haul back to his house, he found an empty spot on a shaded bench and pulled his earnings out of his pockets.

He counted once. He counted twice. Very slowly.

He had made sixty-five dollars. The cups and lemonade mix had cost nine dollars. When he added in his earnings from Wednesday and Thursday, he had one hundred and three dollars and eleven cents.

Now that's *enough,* he thought.

Chapter 8
Going Global

global (glō′bəl) adj. Throughout the world; refers to expanding one's market beyond the immediate area of production.

On Saturday morning, Jessie slept in. And even when she opened her eyes—at 9:05!—she still felt tired. *How can I wake up tired?* she wondered as she buried her face in her pillow and dozed off.

Five minutes later she was awake for real, remembering why she was so tired. Yesterday's lemonade stand had been the hardest work of her life. Face painting, hair braiding, nail polishing—it had sounded like such a good idea. Jessie had been sure that every kid in the neighborhood would line up to buy a cup of lemonade.

But that was the problem. Every kid *had* lined up for lemonade—and then wanted face painting *and* hair braiding *and* fingernail polishing *and* toenail polishing. One boy had asked for face paintings on both cheeks, both arms, and his stomach. One girl begged for lots of little braids with ribbons woven in. And the nail polishing! They all wanted different colors and decals, and it was impossible to get them to sit still long enough for the polish to dry.

"We're going to run out of lemonade," Megan had said to Jessie at noon, as the line stretched all the way to the street.

"Pour half-cups instead of full ones," whispered Jessie. "It has to last."

Jessie and Megan had each made twenty-four dollars on lemonade, but they'd worked eight hours to do it. At the end of the day, they'd agreed: A good idea, but *not worth it!*

After breakfast, Jessie pulled out her lock box and sat on her bed. She kept the box hidden in her closet on a shelf under some sweaters. She kept the key in a plastic box in her desk drawer. The plastic box was disguised to look exactly like a pack of gum. You would never know it was hollow and had a secret sliding panel on its side.

Jessie unlocked the box and opened the lid. First she took out the three torn slips of paper. There was one for *value-added* and one for *goodwill*. There was also a new one that Jessie had added last night:

PROFIT MARGIN: SALES LESS ALL OPERATING COSTS DIVIDED BY THE NUMBER OF SALES. THE RESULT IS A RATIO. FOR EXAMPLE: IF IT COSTS YOU $300 TO MAKE 100 HATS AND YOU SELL THOSE HATS FOR $500, THE PROFIT MARGIN IS: $\frac{500-300}{100} = \frac{2}{1}$

Jessie lined up all three scraps of paper on the bed beside her. She wasn't sure why she was saving these words, but she felt like they belonged in her lock box.

Next, she took out her lemonade earnings. Every day, Megan had squealed over how much money they'd made. But every day, Jessie had known: *It's not enough. It's not going to be enough to win.*

Jessie counted the money. So far, she had earned forty dollars. It was a lot of money. But it wasn't nearly enough. She still needed to earn sixty more dollars. And today was Saturday. Only two more selling days before she and Evan counted their earnings on Sunday night. How was she going to sell enough lemonade to earn sixty dollars in two days?

She couldn't. That was the problem. No kid could earn a hundred dollars in just five days by selling lemonade. The *profit margin* was too small. She knew because she'd used her calculator to figure it out last night.

The numbers said it all. There was no way two girls in one neighborhood could sell 375 cups of lemonade. Nobody wanted *that* much lemonade, no matter how hot the day was.

Jessie looked at the money in her lock box and the page of calculations on her desk. Any other kid would have quit. But Jessie wasn't a quitter. (On

Profit margin for 1 can of lemonade (8 cups):

Sales

8 cups @ 50¢/cup = (8 × .50) = $4.00

Operating costs

Lemonade cost = $1.25

8 paper cups cost = $.15

Total operating costs = $1.40

Number of Sales

8 cups = 8 sales

$$\text{Profit margin} = \frac{\$4.00 - \$1.40}{8}$$

$$= \frac{\$2.60}{8} = \frac{.325}{1}$$

So this means that for every 1 cup of lemonade sold, we earn about 32¢. I get half the profit, and Megan gets half the profit. That means I earn about 16¢ for every cup we sell.

I need to earn $60 to beat Evan.
$60 = 6000¢ (because 60 × 100 = 6000)
So how many times does 16 go into 6000?
6000 ÷ 16 = how many cups I need to sell = 375
I need to sell 375 cups of lemonade! I am DOOMED!!

good days, Jessie's mom called her *persistent*. On bad days, she told her she *just didn't know when enough was enough*.)

Jessie reached for *Ten Bright Ideas to Light Up Your Sales*. It was on her bedside table, right next to *Charlotte's Web*. Jessie's hand hovered. She looked longingly at Wilbur and Fern watching Charlotte hanging by a thread.

But this was war, and she couldn't stop to read for fun.

She grabbed the booklet and opened it to Bright Idea #6.

An hour later, she had a new scrap of paper stashed in her lock box and a whole new page of calculations on her desk. It might work. It *could* work. But she and Megan would have to risk every-thing—*everything* they'd earned over the past three days. And Jessie would have to be braver than she had ever been in her whole life.

Jessie carried her lock box and calculations downstairs. She went into the kitchen and pulled down the school directory, scanning the names of all the third-grade girls from last year. She knew them all—from Evan, from recess, from the lunchroom. Knew who they were. Knew their faces. Which ones were nice. Which ones were not so nice. But she didn't *really* know any of them. Not enough to call them up. Not enough to say, "Want to do something today?" Not enough to ask, "Would you like to have a lemonade stand with me?"

These girls were going to be her classmates. Jessie felt her face grow hot and her upper lip start to sweat. What was it going to feel like to walk into that classroom on the first day of school with all those eyes looking at her? Would they stare? Would they tease? Would they ignore her, even if she said hi?

Jessie looked at the names, then slammed the directory shut. She couldn't do it. She just wasn't brave enough.

Evan walked into the kitchen and grabbed an apple from the fruit bowl. A cloud of fruit flies rose up in the air and settled again. Evan inspected the apple and then bit into it, without washing it first.

Jessie wanted to say something but held her tongue. She looked at him and thought, *It is* never *going to feel normal, not talking to Evan.*

"Hey," she said.

Evan raised his apple to her, his mouth too stuffed to talk.

"So, is Paul coming over today?" she asked.

Evan shook his head, munching noisily.

"Well, is anyone coming over?" Jessie was curious to see what the enemy was up to today. Yesterday, Evan's smile had told her plenty: He had sold a lot of lemonade. A *lot*. But what was he going to do today?

Evan shrugged his shoulders. He swallowed so hard it looked like he was choking down an ocean liner.

"But you *are* setting up a stand, right?" asked Jessie.

"Nah. I'm good," said Evan, looking closely at his apple. "I'm just gonna take it easy today." He took another enormous bite and walked out of the kitchen and down the basement stairs.

Take it easy? How could he take it easy? You didn't take it easy when you were in the middle of a war.

Unless.

Unless he had already won the war.

Could that be possible?

It was impossible!

There was no way Evan had earned a hundred dollars in just three days of selling lemonade. *No way*.

Jessie's mind skittered like one of those long-legged birds on the beach. Had he? Could he? Were her calculations wrong? Was there some other way? Had she overlooked some detail? Some trick? Was she missing something?

Jessie flipped open the school directory. Maybe he had a hundred dollars. Maybe he didn't. She couldn't take a chance. She started putting pencil check marks next to the names of girls she thought might work out.

She'd gone over the list twice when the doorbell rang. It was Megan.

"I've got a new idea," said Jessie.

"Awww, not more lemonade," said Megan, sinking onto the couch in the family room. "I'm tired of selling lemonade. And it's just too hot. I practically had sunstroke yesterday painting all those faces."

"We're done with that," said Jessie. "No more extra services. Doesn't pay off. But here's an idea—"

"Forget lemonade! Let's go to the 7-Eleven," said Megan. "Is Evan home? We could all go."

"No. He's not home," said Jessie, eyeing the door to the basement. She needed Megan to be on board with her plan. She needed Megan to make the phone calls. "Look. This is great. And *we* don't need to sell the lemonade."

Jessie laid out all the details. She showed Megan the new scrap of paper.

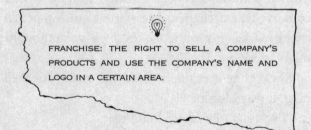

FRANCHISE: THE RIGHT TO SELL A COMPANY'S PRODUCTS AND USE THE COMPANY'S NAME AND LOGO IN A CERTAIN AREA.

Then she showed Megan her page of calculations. At first Megan buried her head under a pillow, but then she poked her head out like a turtle and started to listen for real.

"That sounds like a pretty good plan," she said. "But is it really going to work?"

Jessie looked at her calculations. She'd done them twice. "It should," she said. "I really think it should." She frowned, suddenly not so sure of herself. "It's a big up-front investment. And a lot of work organizing everybody. But once they're set up, we should just be able to sit back and watch the money roll in. The key is spreading everybody out so there'll be plenty of customers. We'll need at least ten girls. Fifteen would be better."

"That's the whole fourth-grade class," said Megan, looking doubtful. "How are we gonna get them to do this?"

"Well, you could phone them all up," said Jessie. She handed Megan the school directory, open to the third-grade page.

"Me?" said Megan. "Why me?"

"Because they know you," said Jessie.

"They know you, too."

"Yeah, but they *like* you."

Megan shook her head. "Not all these girls are my friends."

"Even the ones that aren't your friends, they still like you. *Everybody* likes you, Megan."

Megan looked embarrassed. "Oh, everybody likes you, too," she said.

"No, they don't," said Jessie. "They really don't." There was an uncomfortable silence between the two girls. Then Jessie shrugged her shoulders and said, "I don't know why those girls in my class last year didn't like me. I'm hoping this year will be better."

Megan tapped her fingers on her knees. "You're nervous, huh? About fourth grade?" she asked.

Jessie thought hard. "I'm worried that I won't make any new friends," she said. "You know, that all the kids will think I'm just some puny second-grader and that"—she took a deep breath—"I don't belong."

Megan looked up at the ceiling for a minute. "Do you have an index card?" she asked.

"Huh?"

"I need an index card," said Megan. "Do you have one?"

Jessie went to the kitchen desk and got an index card. She handed it to Megan. Megan started to write something on the card.

"What are you doing?" asked Jessie.

"I'm writing a comment card," said Megan. "That's something you're going to miss from third grade. We did it every Friday. We each got assigned a person, and you had to write something positive about that person on an index card. Then it got read out loud." She folded up the card and handed it to Jessie.

Jessie unfolded the card and read what Megan had written.

You're a really nice person and you have good ideas all the time. You're fun to be with and I'm glad you're my friend.

Jessie stared at the index card. She kept reading the words over and over. "Thanks," she whispered.

"You can keep it," said Megan. "That's what I did. I've got all my comment cards in a basket on my desk. And whenever I'm feeling sad or kind of down on myself, I read through them. They really help me feel better."

Jessie folded the index card and put it in her lock box. She was going to save it forever. It was like having a magic charm.

"So, how about I make half the phone calls and you make the other half?" said Jessie.

"Okay," said Megan, jumping up from the couch.

It was surprising how many almost–fourth-grade girls had absolutely nothing to do three days before school started. In less than an hour, Jessie and Megan had thirteen lemonade "franchises" signed up for the day.

The rest of the day was work, but it was fun. Jessie and Megan attached the old baby carrier to Megan's bike, then rode to the grocery store and spent every penny of their earnings on lemonade mix—fifty-two cans. They actually bought out the store. The four bags of cans filled the carrier like a boxy baby. They also bought five packages of paper cups. When they got back to Megan's house, Jessie tucked the receipt in her lock box, right next to her comment card. Jessie liked receipts: They were precise and complete. A receipt always told the whole story, right down to the very last penny.

```
            Salisbury Farms
    Your Neighborhood Grocery Store
            232 Central Ave.
          09/01/07   11:42AM

Store  23                Trans   246
Wkstn  sys5002          Cashier  KD68VW
Cashier's Name          James
Stock Unit Id           SIAJAMES
Phone Number            800-555-1275


Tastes Right Lemonade
      (52 @ 1.25)                   65.00

Pixie paper Cups
      (5 @ 2.85)                    14.25

Subtotal                            79.25
Tax                                  0.75
Total                               80.00

Cash                                80.00
Change due
  Cash                               0.00

Number of items sold: 57

    Get all your back-to-school supplies
            at Salisbury Farms.
              Happy Labor Day!
```

Then they tossed construction paper and art supplies into the carrier and started making the rounds.

First stop, Salley Knight's house. She was ready for them with a table, chair, and empty pitcher all set up. Jessie mixed the lemonade, Megan quickly made a "Lemonade for sale—75¢ a cup" sign, and they left Salley to her business. The deal was that Salley got to keep one-third of the profits and Jessie and Megan got to keep the rest.

After they'd set up all thirteen lemonade stands, each with enough mix to make four pitchers of lemonade, Jessie and Megan hung out at Megan's house, baking brownies and watching TV. Then they hopped on their bikes again and made the rounds.

Jessie and Megan stopped in front of Salley's house first. The lemonade stand was nowhere to be seen.

"Whaddya think is going on?" asked Megan. Jessie had a bad feeling in her stomach. Something must have gone wrong.

They rang the doorbell. Salley came to the door.

"Hurry," she said, grabbing their arms and pulling them inside. "My mom goes totally mental when the AC is on and the door is open."

"Where's your stand?" asked Jessie nervously, feeling goose bumps ripple up her arms because of the suddenly cool air.

Salley waved her hand. "Done," she said. "I sold out in, like, half an hour. It's so darn hot. We made twenty-four dollars, besides tips. Do I get to keep the tips?"

"Sure," said Jessie. Tips! She'd forgotten about those on her calculations page. Salley handed Jessie some crumpled bills and an avalanche of coins: eight dollars for Jessie and Megan, *each*.

"You wanna stay and have some ice cream?" Salley asked.

"Okay," said Megan. "And we brought you a thank-you brownie. You know, for being part of our team." That had been Bright Idea #9.

After a bowl of The Moose Is Loose ice cream, Jessie and Megan headed out. The story was the same at every girl's house: The lemonade had sold out quickly and the money just kept rolling in.

"I can't believe we made—how much did we make?" squealed Megan once they got back to her house.

"One hundred and four dollars each. *Each!*" shouted Jessie. She couldn't stop hopping from one foot to the other.

"I've never seen so much money in my life!"

Jessie was already running numbers in her head. Subtracting the eighty dollars that she and Megan had spent on lemonade and cups, each girl had made a profit of sixty-four dollars. If they increased the number of franchises from thirteen to twenty-six, they could each make one hundred and twenty-eight dollars in one day. If they ran the twenty-six franchises every day for one week, they could each make eight hundred and ninety-six dollars! Jessie pulled out a piece of paper and scribbled a graph.

The sky was the limit!

Megan pretended to faint when Jessie showed her the graph. "What are you going to do with your money?" she asked from the floor.

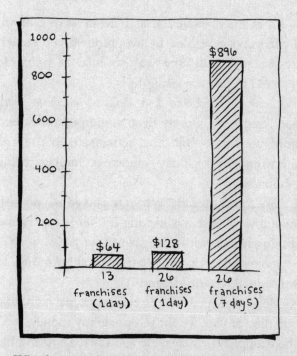

Win the war! thought Jessie. Oops. She couldn't say *that* to Megan. Megan didn't even know about the Lemonade War. After all, Megan *liked* Evan.

Jessie suddenly wondered, *If Megan knew about the war, whose side would she be on?*

All at once, Jessie felt as if Evan were a hawk, circling above, waiting to swoop down and snatch Megan away. Oh, she was so mad at him! He deserved to lose *everything*.

Is one hundred and four dollars enough to win? wondered Jessie. Surely Evan couldn't have earned more than *that*. Still . . . better safe than sorry. She would work all day tomorrow, Sunday, selling lemonade.

"So?" said Megan. "What are you gonna do with the money?" She was kicking off her sneakers and fanning herself with a magazine.

Jessie said, "I'm going to donate all my money to the Animal Rescue League."

Megan stopped waving the magazine. "Oh, that is *so* nice of you. I want to donate my money, too." She dropped the magazine and started shoving her money toward Jessie. "Here. Give mine to the Animal Rescue League, too. On the card, just put both our names."

The money came at her so fast, Jessie didn't know what to say. There it was. Two hundred and eight dollars. Two hundred and eight dollars! All in her hands.

She had won. She had really and truly won the Lemonade War.

"Just promise me one thing," said Megan. "No lemonade stand tomorrow! Okay?"

"O-*kay*," said Jessie. She didn't need a lemonade stand on Sunday if she had two hundred and eight dollars today!

"My dad said tomorrow's the last day before the heat breaks," said Megan. "So we're going to the beach for the whole day. Wanna come?"

"Sure!" said Jessie.

"Maybe Evan wants to come, too?" said Megan.

Jessie shook her head. "No. Evan's busy all day tomorrow. He told me he's got plans."

Megan shrugged. "Too bad for him."

"Yep," said Jessie, thinking of all that money. "Too bad for him."

Chapter 9
Negotiation

negotiation (nĭ-gō′shē-ā′shən) n. A method of bargaining so that you can reach an agreement.

Evan looked up from the marble track he was building when Jessie walked in the front door. She looked hot. She looked sweaty. She looked . . . happy. Really happy. Like she'd just gotten an A+. Or like . . . like she'd just won a war.

"What are you smiling for?" asked Evan, holding a marble at the top of the track.

"No reason." Jessie put her hands on her hips and stared at Evan. She looked like one of those goofy yellow smiley faces—all mouth.

"Well, quit looking at me, would ya? It's creepifying. You look like you're going to explode or something." Evan dropped the marble into the funnel. It raced through the track, picking up speed around the curves. It passed the flywheel, sending the flags spinning, then fell into the final drop. When it reached the end of the track it went sailing through the air like a beautiful silver bird.

And fell short.

The marble landed on the ground, instead of in the bull's-eye cup.

Evan muttered under his breath and adjusted the position of the cup.

"Raise the end of the track," said Jessie. "You'll get more loft."

Evan looked at her angrily. The marble had fallen into the cup the last ten times he'd done it. Why did it have to fall short the one time *she* was watching? "Don't tell me what to do," he said. Why was she smiling like that?

"I didn't tell you what to do," she said. "I just made a suggestion. Take it or leave it." She turned to walk up the stairs. "Grumpminster Fink," she tossed over her shoulder.

Evan threw a marble at her disappearing back but missed by a mile. Well, he hadn't really been aiming anyway; he just wanted that feeling of throwing something. He'd been feeling the need to throw something these past four days.

Grumpminster Fink. That was the name of a character he'd made up when he was six and Jessie was five. That was back when Mom and Dad were fighting a lot and Evan and Jessie just had to get out of the house. They'd scramble up the Climbing Tree—Evan had his branch, Jessie had hers—and wait it out. Sometimes they had to wait a long time. And once, when Jessie was thirsty and impatient and cranky, Evan had said, "Be quiet and I'll tell you a story about Grumpminster Fink."

Grumpminster Fink was a man who was cranky and mean and made everybody miserable. But deep down, he wanted people to love him. It's just that every time he tried to do something nice, it turned out all wrong. Evan had made up a lot of stories about Mr. Fink in that tree. But after Dad left, there just weren't any more stories to tell.

No one in the whole world, besides Jessie and Evan, knew about Grumpminster Fink. And Evan hadn't thought about him in years.

"Hey!" he said sharply. He heard Jessie stop at the top of the stairs, but she didn't come down.

"Do you want to call this whole thing off?" he asked.

"What?" she shouted.

"This . . . this . . . Lemonade War," he said.

"Call it off?"

"Yeah," he said. "Just say nobody wins and nobody loses."

Jessie walked down the stairs and stood with her arms crossed.

Evan looked at her.

He missed her.

He had spent the whole day—the third to last day before school started—by himself. It stunk. It totally stunk. If Jessie had been around—and they hadn't been fighting with each other—they could have played air hockey or made pretzels or built a marble track with twice as many gizmos that launched the marble into the bull's-eye cup every time. Jessie was very precise. She was good at getting the marble to go into the cup.

"Whaddya say?" he asked.

Jessie looked puzzled. "I don't know . . ." she said, frowning. "You see, Megan kinda, well, she . . ."

Evan felt his face go hot. Megan Moriarty. Every time he thought of her his throat got all squeezed and scratchy. It was like the allergic reaction he had if he accidentally ate a shrimp.

"You told Megan Moriarty about—*everything?*" he asked, feeling itchy all over.

"No. Well . . . what 'everything'?" asked Jessie. Evan thought she looked like a fish caught in a net.

"You did." And suddenly Evan knew exactly why Jessie had been smiling when she walked in the door. And why she didn't want to call off the war. She had done it. Again. She had figured out some way to show the world just how stupid he was. Like the time he'd come home with 100 percent on his weekly spelling quiz—the *only* time he'd ever gotten every word right—to find that Jessie had won a statewide poetry-writing contest. He'd thrown his paper into the trash without even telling his mom. What was the point?

Evan didn't know how, but somehow Jessie'd found a way to earn more than one hundred and three dollars. She was going to beat him. And Megan Moriarty knew all about it. And she would tell everyone else. All the girls would know. Paul would know. And Ryan. And Adam and Jack.

Scott Spencer would know. *Can you believe it? He lost to his little sister. The one who's going to be in our class. What a loser!*

"You know what?" he said, pushing past her. "Forget it! Just forget I said anything. The war is on. O-N. Prepare to die."

Chapter 10
malicious mischief

malicious mischief (mə-lĭsh′əs mĭs′chĭf) n. The act of purposely destroying the property of someone else's business.

Jessie was all in knots. Evan was madder than ever at her, and she couldn't figure out why. He had said, "Do you want to call off the war?" and she had said, "Sure, let's call off the war." Or *something* like that. That's what she'd meant to say. That's what she'd *wanted* to say.

But what had she *really* said? She'd mentioned Megan. Oh! She'd almost spilled the beans about Megan giving her the $104. But she hadn't! She'd kept her mouth shut, just in time.

Jessie smiled, remembering that.

So why had Evan acted like that? What was the matter with him?

Jessie lay down on her bed. The world was a confusing place, and she needed Evan to help her figure it out. If this is what fourth grade was going to be like, she might as well just give up now.

And there was something else that was tying her up in knots. That two hundred and eight dollars—it wasn't *really* hers. Megan had given it to her to make a donation. She hadn't given it to Jessie the way Evan's friends had given their money to him. (That still made her so mad when she thought about it. Oh, she wanted to get even with him for saying she didn't have friends!) So even though it looked like she had two hundred and eight dollars in her lock box, only half of that was money she could honestly call her own.

Still . . . if push came to shove and she needed it all to win—

Sure, she'd use it all! This was a war!

But if she pretended that all the money was hers—

Hey, what if Evan has even more than that?

So if she lost, even *with* Megan's money—

Gulp!

Jessie hadn't thought of that. If she lost, even with two hundred and eight dollars. If she lost. *Oh my gosh. Winner takes all.* She would lose all of Megan's money to Evan. How could Jessie explain that to her friend? *You see, I took all the money you earned to help rescue animals and I lost it to my brother, who's going to buy an iPod.* Megan would hate her. All the girls who were friends with Megan would hate her. And Evan already hated her. So that was that. Goodbye, fourth grade.

She couldn't use Megan's money to try to win the bet. It was too risky. But did she have enough to win on her own?

Jessie felt desperation rise in her throat. How much money did Evan have? She had to find out.

Jessie tiptoed upstairs to the attic office. She listened at the closed door. Her mother was on the phone. Then Jessie snuck downstairs. Evan was watching TV in the family room. Like a whisper, she crept back upstairs. And into Evan's room.

There was a strict rule in the Treski house: No one was allowed in anyone else's room without an *express invitation*. That was the term. It meant that Jessie had to say, "Evan, can I come into your room?" and Evan had to say, "Yes," before she put even one toe over the line.

So even though Evan's door was wide open, just crossing the threshold was a direct violation that carried a fine of one dollar. But that was the least of Jessie's concerns.

She snuck over to Evan's bookshelf and picked up a carved cedar box—Evan's chosen souvenir from the family summer vacation. The orange-red wood of the box had a scene etched into the top: a sailboat sailing past a lighthouse while gulls flew overhead. The words "Bar Harbor, Maine" were painted in the sky. The box had brass hinges and a clever latch. What it didn't have was a lock.

Jessie flipped open the lid, immediately smelling the spicy, sharp scent of the wood. She couldn't believe her eyes.

Her hands started pawing through the bills. Dozens of them. There was a ten and a bunch of fives and more ones than she could count. She sat on Evan's bed and quickly sorted out the money.

Evan had one hundred and three dollars and eleven cents.

Eighty-nine cents less than she had.

Eighty-nine cents. He could sell one lousy cup of lemonade tomorrow and beat her. And there was nothing she could do about it because she'd be at the beach.

I can't let him win, she thought. *I can't.* She had gotten to the point where she couldn't even remember what had started the whole war. She couldn't remember why it had been so important to win in the first place. Now she just had to win.

She messed up the money and stuffed it back into the box.

That night in bed, she lay awake trying to think of some way to stop Evan from selling even a single glass.

Sometimes in the dark, dark thoughts come. Jessie had a very dark thought.

The next morning was Sunday, and the rule in the Treski house was that everyone could sleep in as late as he or she wanted. But Jessie awoke to the sound of the electric garage door opening. She sat up in bed and checked the clock: 8:00 a.m. Then she looked out her window just in time to see Evan pedaling away on his bike, his backpack on his back. She quickly dressed and hurried down to the kitchen.

Her mom was making scrambled eggs and toast. "Hi, Jess. Want some?" she asked, pointing with her spatula at the pan of sizzling eggs.

"No, thanks," said Jessie.

"I washed your blue bathing suit last night. It's hanging in the basement. What time are the Moriartys picking you up?"

"Nine o'clock," said Jessie. "Mom, where did Evan go?"

"He went to the store to buy some lemonade

mix." Jessie's mom scooped the eggs onto a plate and put the pan in the sink. When she turned on the faucet, the pan hissed like an angry snake. A great cloud of steam puffed into the air and then disappeared. "What's going on, Jess? What's with all the lemonade stands and you and Evan fighting?"

Jessie opened the pantry cupboard and pulled out a box of Kix. "Nothing," she said. She watched the cereal very carefully as she poured. She didn't want to look at her mother right then.

Mrs. Treski got the milk out of the refrigerator and put it on the counter next to Jessie's bowl. "It doesn't seem like nothing. It seems like there's a lot of bad feeling between the two of you."

Jessie poured her milk slowly. "Evan's mad at me." *And he's going to be a whole lot madder after today*, she added in her head.

"What's he mad about?" asked Mrs. Treski.

"I dunno. He called me a baby and said I ruin everything. And . . ." Jessie felt it coming. She tried to hold it back, but she knew it was coming. Her shoulders tightened up, her chest caved in, and her mouth opened in a howl. "He said he hates me!" Tears poured out of her eyes and dropped into her cereal bowl. Her nose started to run and her lips quivered. With every sob, she let out a sound like tires squealing on a wet road.

For the whole time Jessie cried, her mother wrapped her in a hug. And then, like a faucet turned off, Jessie stopped.

She had told the truth; she really *didn't* understand why Evan was so angry. Even before the Lemonade War he had been mad, and Jessie still didn't know why.

"Better?" asked Mrs. Treski.

"Not much," said Jessie. She wiped her nose with her paper napkin and started eating her cereal. It was soggy, but thankfully not salty.

"Don't you think it would be a good idea to find out what he's mad about?" asked Jessie's mom. "You're never going to stop being mad at each other until you both understand what the other person is feeling."

"I guess so," said Jessie.

"It can be hard. Sometimes it's even hard to know what you're feeling yourself. I mean, how do you feel about *him?*" asked Mrs. Treski.

Jessie didn't have to think long. All the insults and anger, the confusion and fighting, seemed to converge in a single flash of white-hot feeling. "I hate him! I hate him for saying all those mean things. And for not letting me play. I hate him just as much as he hates me. More!"

Mrs. Treski looked sad. "Can we have a sit-down about this tonight? After you get back from the beach?"

"No," said Jessie, remembering the spit vow. Evan would be mad if he knew that she had worried Mom with their fighting. And then he'd spill the beans about the terrible thing she was about to do. Jessie didn't want her mom knowing anything about that. "We'll work it out ourselves, Mom. I promise. Evan and I will talk tonight."

"I'm sorry I've been working so hard," said Mrs. Treski. "I know it's a lousy end to the summer."

"It's okay, Mom. You gotta work, right?"

"Yes. No. I don't know. I promise I'll be finished

by dinnertime tonight. That way we can all go to the fireworks together." Jessie's mom looked out the window. "I hope they don't get canceled because of weather. They're saying scattered thunderstorms this evening."

Jessie and her mom finished breakfast without saying much else.

"I'll clean up," said Jessie. She liked to do dishes, and she wanted to do something nice for her mom.

While she cleaned, she thought about the terrible plan she had come up with last night. It was mean. It was really mean. It was the meanest thing she had ever imagined doing.

I'm not going to do it, she decided. *I hate him, but I don't hate him* that *much.*

She was putting the last glass in the dishwasher when Evan walked in. His backpack was bulging.

"I thought you were going to the beach for the whole day," he said.

"Megan's picking me up in half an hour." She thought she saw Evan stiffen up. *Good.* "What's in the backpack?"

"Not much," he said, dumping out the contents

onto the kitchen table. Cans of lemonade mix rolled all over. Jessie tried to count, but there were too many. Fifteen? Twenty?

"Holy macaroni! How many cans did you buy?"

"Thirty-two." Evan started to stack the cans in a pyramid.

"But, but, you don't need that much. Even to win, you don't need that much. That's, that's—" She did the calculations in her head. "That's two hundred and fifty-six cups of lemonade. If you sell them at fifty cents apiece—"

"A dollar. I'm going to charge a dollar apiece."

Jessie felt like her head was going to explode. "You'll never sell it all," she said. "There isn't a neighborhood in town that will buy two hundred and fifty-six cups in one day." *Too much lemonade. Not enough thirsty people,* she thought.

"I'm going to roll! Like the ice cream truck! I'm going to mix it all up in the big cooler and wagon it from street to street. The high today is going to be ninety-four degrees. It might take me all day, but I'll sell every last drop. *Two hundred and fifty-six smackers!*

And then tonight, Juicy, we count our earnings. Don't forget: Winner takes all!"

"But you don't need two hundred and fifty-six dollars to win!" she shouted.

Evan stood tall and said in that gravelly voice that all the boys imitated, "I don't play to win. I play to *pul-ver-ize*."

Oh! What an idiot! Jessie couldn't believe her brother could be such a jerk. She watched as Evan put together his rolling lemonade stand in the garage. The big cooler was something Mrs. Treski had bought a few years back when she was in charge of refreshments for the school Spring Fling. It looked like a giant bongo drum with a screw-off top and a spigot at the bottom. Evan loaded it into the wagon, then poured in the mix from all thirty-two cans. He used the garden hose to fill the cooler to the top, then dumped in four trays of ice cubes. With a plastic beach shovel, he stirred the lemonade. The ice cubes made a weird rattling noise as they swirled around in the big drum. Using the shovel like a big spoon, he scooped out a tiny bit and tasted it. "Perfect!" he announced, screwing the top on tightly. Then he went into the basement to make his Lemonade-on-Wheels sign.

Without a moment's hesitation, Jessie sprang into action.

First she got out a large Ziploc bag from the kitchen drawer, the kind that you could freeze a whole gallon of strawberries in if you wanted to. Then she held it, upside down and wide open, over the fruit bowl. She gave the bowl a solid knock. Jessie was surprised how easy it was to catch the fruit flies that floated up from the bowl. It was like they wanted to die!

She filled that bag and two more with flies, then hurried to the garage. She unscrewed the top of the big cooler. Holding the first bag upside down, she unzipped it, expecting the flies to fall down into the lemonade. They didn't. They stayed safe and dry in the bag. It was like they wanted to live!

"Too bad for you, you stupid flies," said Jessie as she plunged the bag into the lemonade. Under the surface, she turned the bag inside out, swishing it back and forth so that all the flies were washed off into the lemonade. She emptied all three bags of flies into the big cooler, then hunted around until she found two green inchworms and a fuzzy gypsy moth caterpillar. She tossed them into the cooler. Then she threw in a fistful of dirt, for good measure. She was just about to screw the top back on when she heard Evan coming up the basement stairs. There wasn't time to get the top back on! He would see the bugs and the whole plan would be ruined!

Jessie ran to the steps and shouted, "Evan, Mom wants to see you in her office. Right away!"

"Aw, man," muttered Evan as he started to climb the second set of stairs.

Jessie quickly screwed on the cap, grabbed her blue bathing suit from the basement, then went upstairs to her room. On the way, she passed Evan coming down.

"Mom did *not* want to see me," he said, annoyed.

Jessie looked surprised. "That's what it sounded like. She yelled something down the stairs. I thought it was 'Get Evan.'" Jessie shrugged. "So I got you."

From her bedroom window, she watched Evan rolling down the street with his Lemonade-on-Wheels stand. He was like one of those old-time peddlers, calling out, "Lemonade! Git yer ice-cold lemonade here!" as he walked. For one lightning-brief second, Jessie felt a stab of regret. She could see how hard he was straining to pull the heavy cooler. She knew what it was like to stand in the hot sun selling lemonade. But the feeling was snuffed out by the hurricane of anger she felt when she remembered Evan's gravelly voice: *"pul-ver-ize."*

Jessie switched into her bathing suit, packed up her beach bag, and said a quick goodbye to her mother as the Moriartys pulled into the driveway.

"What a great day for the beach," said her mother. "Have fun. And be home in time for the fireworks, okay?"

The fireworks. Yep. Jessie imagined there would be some fireworks tonight.

Chapter 11
A Total Loss

total loss (tōt′l lôs) n. Goods so damaged that there's no point in repairing them (or they can't be repaired at all).

The first cup was an easy sell.

The second cup, too.

It was on the third cup that a little girl, about six years old, said, "Ew, there's a bug in my drink."

Then her brother said, "There's one in mine, too."

"Gross," said an older boy on a skateboard. "There are, like, three in mine. I want my money back, man," he said, dumping his lemonade on the ground.

The mother of the little girl and boy looked into

their cups carefully. "I think you need to check your lemonade, honey," she said to Evan.

Evan unscrewed the cap and everyone looked in. The surface was swimming with dead bugs: fruit flies, worms, and a soggy brown caterpillar.

"Oh my goodness," said the mother.

The boy started spitting on the ground like he was going to die. The girl started wailing. "Mommy! I drank bugs. I have bugs in my tummy!"

Evan couldn't believe his eyes. How did this happen? Did they crawl in somehow? They couldn't have. He had screwed the lid on tightly. He was sure of it. And anyway . . . one or two bugs crawling in— maybe. But fifty dead fruit flies and two inchworms and a caterpillar? It just wasn't possible.

Evan was burning with embarrassment as everyone looked at him and his buggy lemonade. Frantically, he reached into the cooler and started to scoop out the dead bugs with his hands.

"Uh, sweetheart," said the mother, "you can't sell that lemonade."

"I'll get them all," said Evan. "I'll get every last one out."

"No, dear. You really can't. You need to dump it out," she said.

Evan looked at her like she was crazy. Dump it out? *Dump it out?* He'd spent forty dollars of his hard-earned money on that lemonade and another dollar for the cups. He wasn't going to dump it out.

"I'll do it at home," he said.

"No. You should do it here, I think. I need to be sure it's all disposed of properly."

Evan looked at her. He didn't know her, but he knew her type. Boy, did he know her type. She was the kind of mother who thought she was the mother of the whole world. If you were on a playground and she thought you were playing too rough, she'd tell you. If you were chewing gum in line at the 7-Eleven, she'd say, "I sure hope that's sugarless." Mothers like that never minded just their own business. Or just their kids' business. They thought they had to take care of every kid in the kingdom.

"It's too heavy for me to dump," he said. "I'll take it home and my mom can help."

"*I'll* help," said the busybody mother of the world. "All we need to do is tip it a little." She grabbed one handle of the big cooler. Evan had no choice but to grab the other handle. Together they tipped and the lemonade poured out of the top of the cooler.

They poured and poured and poured. The lemonade sparkled in the sunlight, like a bejeweled waterfall, and then disappeared without a trace, soaking into the parched September grass. As the last sluice of lemonade slipped out of the cooler, a slick of mud poured out.

"Oh my goodness," said the mother.

Evan couldn't believe it. He couldn't believe how quickly his victory had turned to defeat. It was just like the lemonade. It had disappeared into the grass, leaving nothing behind. A total loss.

The mother smiled sympathetically as Evan returned her two dollars. The skateboard dude had already skated off with his refund. There was nothing to do but go home.

Evan walked slowly, dragging the wagon with the empty cooler rattling inside.

With every step he took, the wagon handle

poked him in the rear end. Step. Poke. Step. Poke. He felt like someone was nudging him forward.

"Evan, Mom wants to see you in her office. Right away!"

That had been weird. His mom had had no idea what he meant. "I didn't call you. I didn't call anyone," she had said. "I've been on the computer."

"Evan, Mom wants to see you."

He had been coming up the stairs. Jessie had been in the garage. She had looked anxious. *"Right away!"* she had said.

Evan stopped walking. He stared at the empty cooler. Then he started to run. The wagon bounced crazily along the uneven sidewalk. Twice it tipped over. *What did it matter?* thought Evan angrily. *There's no lemonade to spill.*

By the time he got home, he had it all figured out. He looked in the kitchen trash and found the three Ziploc bags, inside out and sticky with lemonade. He shook the fruit bowl and noticed how few fruit flies took to the air. If he'd had the right materials, he would have dusted the cooler for fingerprints. But there was really no need for that.

He knew what he would have found: Jessie was all over this one.

"That RAT! That lousy rotten stinking RAT of a sister!" he shouted. He went back to the garage and kicked the wagon. He knocked the cooler to the floor. He tore up his Lemonade-on-Wheels sign into a dozen pieces.

He was going to lose. She had a hundred dollars (he was sure of it) and he had just sixty-two left. Tonight, before the fireworks, when they counted their money, she would be the winner and he would be the loser.

Winner takes all.

Loser gets nothing.

It was so unfair.

Evan stomped upstairs to his room. He slammed the door so hard, it bounced open again. When he went to close it, he was staring across the hallway, straight into Jessie's room. He could see her neatly made bed covered in Koosh pillows, the poster of Bar Harbor from their trip to Maine this summer, and her night table with *Charlotte's Web* at the ready.

Evan crossed the hall, then paused at Jessie's door. There was the rule about not entering. Well, *she'd* broken the rules first. (Even though there wasn't really a rule about fruit flies and lemonade, it was clearly a dirty trick.) Evan walked in and went straight to Jessie's desk drawer.

There was the fake pack of gum. Inside, the key. Did she really think he didn't know where she hid it? He'd seen her slip the key inside the box when he was passing by on his way to the bathroom. Jessie was smart, but she wasn't very smooth. He'd known for months where the key was hidden. He just hadn't bothered to use it.

Until now.

It took him a while to find the lock box. He checked the bureau drawers first and then under Jessie's bed. But finally he found it hidden in her closet. Again, not very smooth.

Evan carried the key and the lock box back to his room and sat on the bed. He put the key in the lock and opened the top. Then—the moment of truth—he lifted out the plastic change tray.

There were a whole bunch of scraps of paper on top, and there was a folded index card, too. Evan moved these aside and found a ten-dollar bill paper-clipped to a birthday card. Under that was an envelope labeled "Pre-War Earnings" with four dollars and forty-two cents inside it. That was the money Jessie had had before the Lemonade War began. She'd kept it separate, just like she promised. Next to it was a fat envelope labeled "Lemonade Earnings." Evan opened the envelope.

Inside, the bills were arranged by ones, fives, and tens. All the bills were facing the same way, so that the eyes of George Washington, Abraham Lincoln, and Alexander Hamilton were all looking at Evan as he counted out the cash.

Two hundred and eight dollars.

There it was. The winning wad.

Evan thought of how hard he'd worked that week, in the blazing sun, in the scorching heat. He thought about the coolerful of lemonade pouring into the grass. He thought about handing over his sixty-two dollars and eleven cents to Jessie and how she'd smile and laugh and tell. Tell everyone that she had won the Lemonade War. The guys would all shake their heads. *What a loser*. Megan would turn away. *What a stupid jerk*.

Evan slammed the lid of the lock box shut. He stuffed the envelope in his shorts pocket. He was *not* going to let it happen!

He wasn't planning to keep the money. Not for good. But he wasn't going to let her have it tonight. When it came time to show their earnings, he'd have sixty-two dollars and eleven cents and she'd have *nothing*. He'd give her the money back tomorrow or maybe the day after that, but *not tonight*.

He suddenly felt a desperate need to get out of the house as fast as he could. He shoved the lock box back into Jessie's closet and the key back into the fake pack of gum.

"Hey, Mom," he shouted, not even waiting for her to answer back. "I'm going to the school to see if there's a game. 'Kay?"

Chapter 12
waiting period

waiting period (wāt′tǐng pǐr′ē-əd) n. A specified delay, required by law, between taking an action and seeing the results of that action.

Jessie wanted to have fun. She really did. But it seemed like the more she tried, the less she had.

First, the drive to the beach took two and a half hours because of traffic. Jessie felt the car lurching. Forward, stop. Forward, stop.

"Memo to myself," said Mr. Moriarty. "Never go to the beach on the Sunday of Labor Day weekend. Especially when there's been a heat wave for more than a week."

In the back seat, Jessie and Megan played license

plate tag and magnetic bingo and twenty questions, but by the end of the car ride, Jessie was cramped and bored.

Then the beach parking lot was full, so they had to park half a mile away and walk. Then the beach was so crowded that they could hardly find a spot for their blanket. Then Megan said the water was too cold and she just wanted to go in up to her ankles. She kept squealing and running backwards every time a gentle ripple of a wave came her way.

What fun was that? Sure, the water was cold! It was the North Shore. It was *supposed* to be cold. That's why it felt so good on a hot day like this. When Jessie and Evan went to the beach, they would boogie board and bodysurf and skimboard and throw a Screaming Scrunch Ball back and forth the whole time. They loved to stay in the water until their lips turned blue and they couldn't stop shaking. Then they'd roast themselves like weenies on their towels until they were hot and sweating again, and then they'd go right back in. Now *that* was fun at the beach.

Megan liked to build sandcastles and collect

shells and play sand tennis and read magazines. *That's all fine,* thought Jessie. *But not going in the water? That's crazy.*

The ride home was itchy and hot. Jessie had sand in all the places where her skin rubbed together: between her toes, behind her ears, and between the cheeks of her bottom. And somehow she'd gotten sunburned on her back, even though Mrs. Moriarty had smeared her all over with thick, goopy sunscreen twice. Jessie didn't even have the patience for ten questions, let alone twenty.

But Megan didn't get that Jessie didn't feel like talking. She kept trying to get her to take a quiz in a teen magazine. If Evan had been there, he would have kept quiet. Or maybe hummed a little. Jessie liked it when Evan hummed.

As they turned onto Damon Road, Megan asked, "Are you feeling sick?"

In fact, she was. For the past half-hour, Jessie had been imagining walking in the door and facing Evan. And she'd been feeling sicker and sicker with every mile that brought her closer to home.

Chapter 13
crisis management

crisis management (krī′sĭs măn′ĭj-mənt) n. Special or extraordinary methods and procedures used when a business is in danger of failing.

"Sucker!"

"Oh, man. You were *schooled!*"

"*Pre*-school, baby!"

For the third time that afternoon, Scott Spencer had gotten the drop on Evan, dribbling around him and then hitting the easy lay-up. So the guys were giving him the business, even the ones on his own team. It was Evan, Paul, and Ryan against Kevin Toomey, Malik Lewis, and Scott. Evan wished that

Scott hadn't shown up, but he had, and they needed the sixth guy for three-on-three since Jack had gone home to ask his mom if they could all swim at his house. So what was Evan supposed to say?

Anyway, Evan was three times the ball handler that Scott was and everyone knew it. So it was all in fun.

But it didn't feel like much fun to Evan.

"What's up, man?" Paul asked.

Evan dribbled the ball back and forth, left hand, right hand, and then through his legs. "Hey, it's hot," he said.

"Yeah, it's hot for all of us," said Paul. "Get your game on, dude."

But Evan couldn't get his moves right. He was a half-step behind himself. And every time he moved, the envelope slapped against his thigh like a reprimand.

"Speaking of hot," said Ryan. Everyone turned to look. Jack was coming up the path, running at a dead-dog pace.

"Oh, please, God," said Paul. "Let her say yes."

As soon as he was in range, Jack shouted, "She said yes!"

"What's up?" asked Scott.

"Jack asked his mom if we could all go swimming in his pool," Kevin said.

"Hey, Jack," shouted Scott. "Can I come, too?"

"Yeah, sure," said Jack, who'd stopped running toward them and was waiting for them to join him on the path.

Oh, great, thought Evan. But he wasn't about to turn down a dunk in a pool just because Scott Spencer would be there.

Nobody wanted to go home for suits and towels. Kevin, Malik, and Ryan were wearing basketball shorts anyway, so they could swim in those. "We've got enough suits at the house," said Jack. "My mom saves all our old ones."

At the house, Evan changed into one of Jack's suits. He wrapped up his underwear and shirt inside his shorts and put the bundle of clothes on the end of Jack's bed next to all the other guys' piled-up clothes. It felt good to drop the heavy shorts with the envelope stuffed in the pocket. Then, just to be sure, he put his shoes on top of his pile of clothes. He didn't want anything happening to that money.

They played pool basketball all afternoon, even though the teams were uneven. Mrs. Bagdasarian brought out drinks and cookies and chips and sliced-up watermelon. Every time one of them went into the house to use the bathroom, she shouted, "Dry off before you come in!" but she did it in a nice way.

Then, just when Evan thought the afternoon couldn't get any better, it did. Scott had gone into the house to go to the bathroom. A few minutes later he came out dressed, his hair still dripping down his back.

"I gotta go," he said, jamming his foot into his sneaker.

"Did your mom call?" asked Ryan.

"Nope, I just gotta go," he said. "See ya." He ran out the gate.

"Great," shouted Evan. "Now the teams are even." And they went back to playing pool hoops. Evan didn't think about Scott Spencer for the rest of the afternoon.

He didn't think about Scott Spencer until he went into Jack's bedroom to change back into his clothes and noticed that his shoes were on the floor and his shorts weren't folded up.

Chapter 14
Reconciliation

reconciliation (rĕk'ən-sĭl'ē-ā'shən) n. The act of bringing together after a difference, as in to reconcile numbers on a balance sheet; resolution.

"Come on, you two," Mrs. Treski called up the stairs. "If we don't go now, there won't be any room on the grass."

"We're coming," shouted Evan, sticking his head out of his room. Jessie was sitting on his bed, and he was trying to get her to go to the fireworks. She had her lock box on her lap and a mulish look on her face.

"Just say it's a tie," said Evan. "C'mon, Jess. This

160

whole thing is stupid and you know it."

"It's not a tie unless it's a tie," said Jessie, knowing she sounded like a brat but not able to stop herself. "How much have you got?"

"Mom's waiting," said Evan. "Put your dumb box away and let's go to the fireworks."

"How much have you got?"

Evan tensed up his fingers as if he were strangling an invisible ghost. "Nothing! Okay? I've got nothing. Look." He turned the pockets of his shorts inside out.

Jessie looked skeptical. "You can't have *nothing*. You must have made *something*."

"Well, I had expenses. So I ended up with nothing. Okay? Are you happy? You win." Evan sat on the edge of the bed, looking at the floor.

Jessie felt her heart sink. "You spent *all* your money on mix for your Lemonade-on-Wheels stand?" Jessie asked. "All of it?"

Evan nodded. Jessie felt like crawling under the bed and never coming out. "It didn't pay off so good?" she whispered.

"There were a few bugs in the system," said Evan. *That's a joke Jessie would have loved,* he thought. Before the war. Now it was all just money and numbers and bad feelings. There was no room for laughing.

"Oh," said Jessie, her voice the size of an ant. She stared down at the box in her lap. "I've got—"

She opened the lid of the lock box, took out the change tray, and pushed aside all the scraps of paper she had collected and the comment card from Megan. She stared. "Wait a minute. This isn't my money." She picked up a handful of wrinkled, bunched-up bills. Evan lay down on the bed and covered his head with his pillow. Jessie counted the money quickly. "Sixty-two dollars and eleven cents? Where'd this come from?"

"Imamummy," said Evan from underneath the pillow.

"What?" said Jessie. "Take that dumb pillow away. I can't understand what you're saying." She hit the side of his leg for emphasis.

"It's my money!" he shouted, still through the

pillow. "It was a hundred and three dollars, but then I spent forty-one dollars for the Lemonade-on-Wheels stand. So now it's just sixty-two."

"Your money? But where's my money?"

Evan pulled the pillow away from his face. His eyes were closed. His nose pointed at the ceiling. He folded his arms across his chest like a dead man. "I took it."

"Well, give it back," said Jessie. This time she hit the side of his leg for real.

"I can't. It's gone." He lay as still as a three-day-old corpse.

"Gone? Gone where?" Jessie was shrieking now. Never in her life had she worked so hard to earn money. Never in her life had she had more than one hundred dollars in her hand. Never in her life had she had a friend who trusted her like Megan had.

"I don't know. It was in my shorts pocket. And then I played basketball with the guys. And then we went to Jack's house to swim. And I took off my shorts and borrowed a suit. And when I went back to change, the money was gone." He sat up and faced his sister. "I'm *really* sorry."

In a real war you fight. You fight with your hands and with weapons. You fight with anything you've got because it's a matter of life and death. Jessie felt the loss of her hard-earned money like a death, and she ripped into Evan with all the power in her body. She punched him. She kicked him. She threw her lock box at him. She wanted to tear him up into little pieces.

Evan didn't try to pin her, though it would have been easy to do. Part of him just wanted to lie on the bed and take it. Take it all. For being the one who started the whole thing by saying, "I hate you." For making Jessie feel so rotten about herself just because Evan felt so rotten about himself. For taking Jessie's money and losing it to Scott. Just for being so stupid.

But Jessie was really going at it, and if he didn't protect himself at least a little, he was going to end up in the emergency room and that would upset his mom. So he kept his hands up in front of his face, just enough to keep Jessie from gouging out his eyes. But he never once tried to hit her back. He was done fighting.

Finally Jessie ran out of gas. She lay down on the bed and tried to make her brain work. Her body was so worn out that her brain felt like the only part of her that *could* work.

"One of your friends stole my money?" she asked.

"I think it was Scott Spencer," said Evan. "He went upstairs to go to the bathroom. And then he came down all in a hurry and said he had to go home. After that, I went upstairs and the money was gone."

"He's such a jerk," said Jessie.

"The biggest," said Evan. "If he gets an Xbox, I'll *know* it was him."

"It was a lot of money," said Jessie, feeling tears start to spring from her eyes and run down her face.

"It *was,*" said Evan. "I couldn't believe how much when I saw it. You're really something, you know that? Earning all that money selling lemonade."

Thanks, thought Jessie, though she couldn't say the word. "Why'd you do it, Evan?" she asked. She meant *Why'd you take the money? And why'd you act so mean? And why'd you start this whole war in the first place?* There were too many questions.

"I was mad at you for putting the bugs in my lemonade," he said.

"Well, I was mad at you for saying you wanted to pulverize me," she said.

"I only did that because you were hanging out with Megan and I felt totally left out."

"Well, how do you think I felt when you wouldn't let me hang out with you and stupid Scott Spencer?"

"Well, I was mad at you because . . . because . . ."

Jessie sat up and looked at Evan. Evan looked at the wall.

"Because I don't want you in my class this year," he said.

"Because I'll embarrass you," she said solemnly.

"Because I'll embarrass *myself*," said Evan. "I never have the right answer in math. And I read slower than everyone when I read out loud. And I make mistakes. All the time. And now with you in

166

the class, it's going to be worse. They'll all say, 'Wow, he's even dumber than his little sister.'" Evan's shoulders slumped and his head hung low.

"You're not dumb," said Jessie.

"I know you don't *think* I am," he said. "And that stinks, too. That you're going to *see* how dumb I am in school."

"You're not dumb," said Jessie again. "You made a hundred and three dollars and eleven cents selling lemonade in just five days."

"Yeah, but you made two hundred and eight dollars! You see? You're my little sister, and you're twice as smart as me."

Jessie shook her head. "Half that money is Megan's. She just gave it to me to give to the Animal Rescue League. I only made a hundred and four dollars."

Evan unslumped. "Really?" Jessie nodded yes. "So you made a hundred and four and I made a hundred and three?"

"And eleven cents," said Jessie.

"So it was really a tie?" said Evan.

"No," said Jessie. "I won. By eighty-nine cents."

"But, I mean, c'mon," said Evan. "After all that, it was *practically* a tie."

"No," said Jessie. "It was close. But I really won."

"Wow, we pretty much tied," said Evan.

Jessie decided to let it go. For the first time in four days, she didn't care about who had more and who had less. Besides, she was waiting to see how long it took before Evan figured *it* out.

Not long.

"Holy crud!" he said suddenly. "I lost Megan's money, too? A hundred and four dollars of her money? Oh, CRUD." He threw himself back on his bed and covered his face with both arms. Neither of them said anything for a long time. Finally Jessie broke the silence.

"I'm really sorry I put the bugs in your lemonade."

"Thanks," said Evan. "I'm sorry I took your and Megan's money."

"We shouldn't have done any of this," Jessie said, waving her hand at the money on the bed.

"It ruined the end of summer."

"Yeah, the whole summer's been crud," said Evan.

"Not the *whole* summer. Just the last five days. Remember we went to Bar Harbor? And we swam at the pond?" Jessie couldn't stand Evan thinking their whole summer together had been crud.

"Yeah, but I think the last five days kind of cancels all that out," said Evan. "I can't believe I have to tell Megan Moriarty—"

"She likes you," said Jessie.

Evan sat up, surprised. "Really?"

"Yeah," said Jessie. "I don't get it either. But she's always asking what you're doing and if you can play and stuff. Why do you think she does that?"

"Cool," said Evan, smiling. "So you guys are friends?"

"Yeah," said Jessie. "We're good friends."

"Okay then. So she'll be coming over here to play and stuff. Right? That's cool."

"You're weird," said Jessie.

"Yes, I am," said Evan.

There was another long silence. The late-summer light in Evan's one-window room had faded to black, but neither one of them wanted to turn on a light. It was nice sitting there, just the two of them, in the cooling darkness. An afternoon breeze had kicked itself into a gusty wind, and the shade on the window tapped out a steady beat that was pleasant and reassuring.

"This war was stupid," said Jessie.

Evan nodded in the dark.

Just then they heard the sound of thunder booming in the distance. Then more and more until the whole house shook.

"The fireworks!" shouted Jessie.

"Oh, snap!" shouted Evan.

Jessie and Evan raced down the stairs. At the bottom, they found their mother sitting on the last step, watching the sky through the sliding screen door.

"Why didn't you call us?" said Evan.

"We're missing the fireworks!" said Jessie.

"Oh, I figured whatever the two of you were talking about was more important than a fireworks show." Mrs. Treski turned to look at her kids. "Did you work it out?"

Evan and Jessie nodded just as a roman candle exploded in the sky.

"Not a bad seat," said Mrs. Treski, patting the step. "Enjoy."

For twenty minutes, the night sky was alive with wagon wheels, party-colored dahlias, and whistling glitter palms. Evan, Jessie, and Mrs. Treski sat watching, silent but for the occasional "Oohhh" and "Aahhh" that seemed to escape from their lips like hissing air from an overblown tire.

When the last of the fireworks bloomed and then faded, Evan, Jessie, and Mrs. Treski sat in the darkness, waiting. No one said anything for several minutes. And then Jessie whispered, "It's over."

Yes. It was over.

"Wait," said Evan. "What was that?"

"What?" asked Jessie, straining her ears.

"Listen."

In the distance, a boom and a rattle.

"More fireworks," said Evan, staring up at the dark sky.

"Where? I don't see them," said Jessie.

All of a sudden the sky split in two as lightning sliced the night. An explosion of thunder rolled through the house, rattling the windows and pictures on the walls. Rain poured from the sky as if a gigantic faucet had been twisted on.

"Yow!" shouted Mrs. Treski, leaping up from the step. "Battle stations!"

Every window in the house was wide open, so Evan, Jessie, and Mrs. Treski ran from the top floor to the bottom, shutting windows and sopping up puddles. The rain came down with the fury and impatience of a two-year-old having a tantrum. As he closed the window in his room, Evan could hear the gurgle of the gutters choking on the downpour.

"One thing ends, another begins," said Mrs. Treski, meeting Jessie and Evan on the stairs. She raised her index finger, like a wise philosopher. "Fireworks. Rainstorm."

Jessie raised her index finger. "Summer. School."

Evan raised his index finger. "War. Peace."

Then they laughed because it was silly—the three of them acting like wise philosophers, standing on the stairs.

That night, before she closed her door, Jessie whisper-shouted to Evan, who was already in bed, "Hey. I've got an idea. About getting Megan's money back."

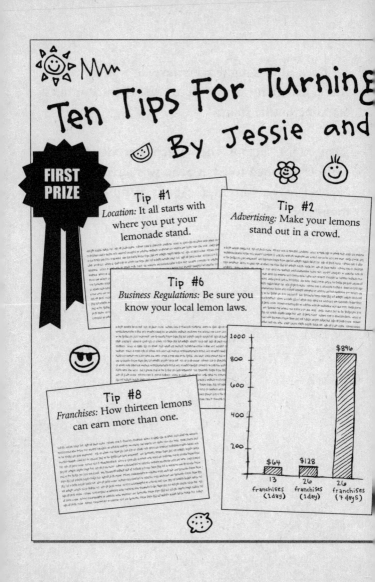

Lemons Into Loot
Evan Treski

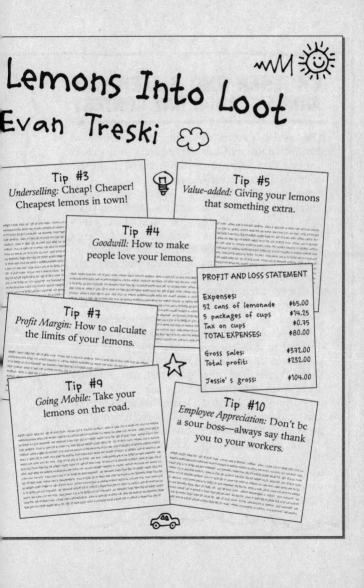

Tip #3
Underselling: Cheap! Cheaper! Cheapest lemons in town!

Tip #5
Value-added: Giving your lemons that something extra.

Tip #4
Goodwill: How to make people love your lemons.

PROFIT AND LOSS STATEMENT

Expenses:	
52 cans of lemonade	$65.00
5 packages of cups	$14.25
Tax on cups	$0.75
TOTAL EXPENSES:	$80.00
Gross sales:	$372.00
Total profit:	$232.00
Jessie's gross:	$104.00

Tip #7
Profit Margin: How to calculate the limits of your lemons.

Tip #9
Going Mobile: Take your lemons on the road.

Tip #10
Employee Appreciation: Don't be a sour boss—always say thank you to your workers.

BROTHER AND SISTER WIN ANNUAL LABOR DAY CONTEST

This year's winners in the annual Rotary Club Labor Day Contest open to all town residents ages 8–12 are Jessie (age 8) and Evan (age 10) Treski of 81 Parsons Road. The brother-and-sister team created an impressive poster that described their entrepreneurial efforts as purveyors of lemonade.

"It was hot, so we decided to sell lemonade," said Evan. "And then Jessie had the great idea of taking everything we learned and making it into a poster for the contest."

The award-winning poster included ten tips for running a successful lemonade stand, a profit-and-loss statement, business definitions, and a chart that tracked franchise profits.

"We've had other entries in other years that described businesses," said Jack Petrocini, president of the local chapter of the Rotary Club. "But never anything with this much detail. We were very impressed."

Jessie and Evan will share the $100 prize money. Will they use it to start up another business? "No," said Jessie. "We kind of need a break from running a business, because of school starting."

Both Jessie and Evan are fourth-graders at Hillside Elementary School.

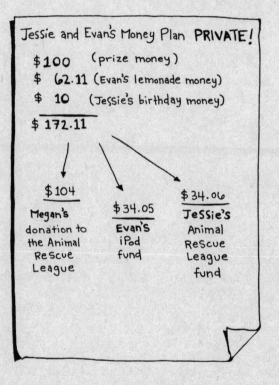

Jessie and Evan's Money Plan **PRIVATE!**

$100   (prize money)

$ 62.11 (Evan's lemonade money)

$ 10   (Jessie's birthday money)

$ 172.11

$104

Megan's
donation to
the Animal
Rescue
League

$34.05

Evan's
iPod
fund

$34.06

Jessie's
Animal
Rescue
League
fund